To Piotr Skrzenecki,
the Wolf,
and the Man in the Black Hole

Malinski

Síofra O'Donovan

THE LILLIPUT PRESS
DUBLIN

First paperback edition, 2001

First published 2000 by
THE LILLIPUT PRESS LTD
62 63 Sitric Road, Arbour Hill,
Dublin 7, Ireland
www.lilliputpress.ie

A CIP record for this title is available from
The British Library.

1 3 5 7 9 10 8 6 4 2

ISBN 1 901866 69 6

*The Lilliput Press receives financial assistance
from An Chomhairle Ealaíon / The Arts Council of Ireland.*

Set in 10.5 on 15.5 Adobe Caslon
Printed in England by MPG Books, Bodmin, Cornwall

I

Stanislav

I

I am an old man now. I live here, on the top floor of a tower block overlooking the Vistula. Since the war, since Mama left. Since the Germans came and the Germans left and the Russians came, scarlet red, and left us grey.

I should have died in the war. Instead, I was preserved. Like my bureau, my wingback chair, my rococo clock. Not much left of the manor, but enough. I sometimes press my cheek against the bureau and hear my father scratching on it with his ivory pen. I lean my ear against the little clock and hear it echo across the wooden floors in Lvov. And I crawl like an insistent louse into the drawers, between the hinges, down the bevelling, where memory has not been erased.

Mama had the chattels sent up to Kraków during the war. I have kept them for her as long as I have kept her pickles in the cellar. Rows of obedient little jars—cherries, onions, herrings, plums that were smuggled past the Third Reich. Do I clutch too much? Mama said I did and maybe that is why I lost her. But I did not lose her, she left me. She left me, they left me. They left without me, the day the Germans came, and they never came back.

2

It is here in this room that I shall greet my brother Henryk, alias Henry, forty-nine years since our parting.

Two years before the Germans came to Lvov, a Russian commission threw us out of our house. It was 1939. We went to live with the peasants. Jozef guarded the family paintings in a barn loft. They slept on their backs for the war, wrapped in linen. I do not know what became of them but I am convinced that I will chance upon them in a museum some day before I die.

There was a portrait of my grandfather. He peered out of the canvas, the manor dangling on the horizon behind him. He was a cautious, patriotic man who despaired over his ever-shrinking estate. The more stubborn his stance on independence from the Tsar, the more was hacked off his estate and handed to the peasants. It was like a large woollen cardigan that would not stop unravelling. By the time my father was born, it was a modest estate. We had no empire furniture, no chandeliers, no ballroom. We had ourselves and our books.

There was another painting: an odd, slanting view of Kazimierz-Dolny. Its perspective was naïve, its brushwork rough and thick. It had an unsettling effect on me. Each of the rickety houses looked as if it might topple down the hill. I did not like that. I had always had a fear of houses toppling over. When scarlet fever took my grandfather, Mama hid the painting in the attic. She thought it crude.

June, 1941. The cuckoo peasants, who for two years had occupied the manor, fled. German panzers prowled around the border. We thought we still had time. Mama brought us back to the manor to fetch her hats and dig up the silver. There was blood on our floorboards. I found Papa's bearskins lying on the beds with their heads propped up against the walls. There were chickens in the dining room and a pig that grunted at us rudely, as if we had intruded. Most of our furniture was there, all scratched and with the stuffing spiralling out of holes in the upholstery. The bureau and the wingback were safe in Kraków in my aunt Magdalena's home.

I could not understand how we had chanced upon this war, or it had chanced upon us, since we had never done a thing but live in a house and eat and sleep and play music and dance and, well, Papa had hunted, but he had never shot a Russian or a German. I stood there with Mama, aghast at what they'd done. Those mindless chickens. That hairy pig. The bloody floor. The ugly rope stretched across the hall with coal-stained linens draped over it.

Mama did not let us see her tears. But I heard her sniffling under the straw hat she'd just stolen back. When I kissed her, she smelt of mildew and I blamed the war. I watched her, trembling across the hall in her hat, like a resurrected lamp-stand. She phaffed at the filthy linens as she stooped to pass them by and led us both by the hand out to the veranda. I looked back at Papa's deer heads, whose bodies, I had always fancied, were cemented into the thick hall walls. Those glass eyes had seen it all. We left them behind, stuck in the walls. That was my last visit to the manor. Never to return. When the Russians came back, our land was collectivized. Ten families moved into the house. The paddocks were ploughed under. The orchards, the fields, the grounds all became part of Kolkzoz no. 187.

Jozef took Mama and Henryk and me away from the manor in his farm cart. We sped past fields of yellow flowers. A stork hovered over us a while, then quit the sky and drowned among the flowers. Mama blessed herself and kissed our hands. She prayed to the sky in Latin. We galloped on and on, our home a sad grey dot behind us.

Little Henryk huddled up beside her legs and cried there. Mama ran her fingers through his hair. I stayed still and I said nothing.

'Mama,' said Henryk, 'are we going to hell? Did we do something wrong?'

'No,' said Mama, 'we're just Polish, Henryk. We are Poles.'

And she stroked his cheek with her damp hand. But I stayed still and I did not take her other hand. Mama praying under her breath, *Jesus, Jesus, Jesus Mary, maybe we are going to hell.* I wonder did you hear it, Henryk.

Jozef's wife gave us borsch and dry bread. We were to take a train to Kraków to my mother's sister's home. But something happened. Henryk: he howled. He howled and stamped his feet and banged his fists on his thighs. He flung his soup on the floor and smashed his dry bread under his boot. When Mama slapped him, he just howled more.

'Jesus Mary what is it? What is it? And you dare to fling your soup on the floor in someone else's home?'

Jozef's wife picked up the bowl and licked it. She put the dry crumbs in it and nibbled at them in the corner, her big eyes fixed on the howling boy.

'I want my red train!' screamed Henryk. He pounded his fist

on the table. 'I want my red train! I will not leave without it!'

He told Mama it was in the attic of the manor, where he'd left it, before the war. Why, Henryk, did you not get it when we went back?

'The pig,' he said. 'The big fat pig. And we were in a hurry and I forgot. The big black pig. It's his fault! It's all his fault! It's not my fault!' And he fell into Mama's lap. He looked up at her with his bewitching little eyes (which were her own), and the wish, war or no war, was granted.

'Jozef, can you bring us back? It's not too far.'

Jozef's face hung under the oil lamp, full of shadows. Surely there would be time, Mama said, before the Germans came, surely they could make it back with the toy train? Really, it wasn't far away. Surely there was time. There was no time, said Jozef, but he'd bring them anyway. Something rumbled in the distance. Jozef got up. He would bring them back. After all, it wasn't very far.

Henryk stood at the far corner of the table, straight-backed and expressionless, awaiting the execution of his order.

'They'll have you hung and shot! Pani Malinska, forgive me, but you are mad.' Mama scowled at Jozef's wife. Another rumble in the distance. A piece of earth, I thought. A piece of earth has fallen. There is a hole in the earth and we will all fall into it. Mama held my face in her hands and kissed my forehead.

'You stay here, Stanislav. You stay here and we'll be back.'

Of course they never came back. I never saw Mama again. That spoilt, collaborating little brat stole my darling Mama and gave her to the Germans. I cannot forgive that child: pouting, slate-eyed, as convinced as the enemy.

Now he is an ageing man, like me. He will come to my apartment. I will greet him at that door, I will take his coat, put his shoes aside, and hand him my spare slippers, as if nothing had ever happened. Henryk, Henry, my brother, my traitor, is coming to visit me after forty-nine years.

I don't pity myself. That's just how it was. War does that and did worse. I still have my body, trampled by history, scratched, bruised, bent a little and home to some interesting deformities. A small lymph node nestles at the foot of my crown. It emerged in 1953. Some teeth are missing. I have them in a pillbox somewhere (I had intended to send them to Mama). The sinew in my right hand has stiffened so that it is virtually inflexible. I have some ingrown toenails that need attending. But none of this merits a visit to the doctor. Oh, I could see a state doctor, but I couldn't endure the queues. I am too tired.

I waited thirty hours in Jozef's home for them to return. His wife boiled socks for the first three hours, baked bread for the next three, slept for six, prayed for two and wept for the rest. She said they had been shot and flung into an open grave in the forest. I would not believe her. I imagined them hiding in the tree-tops, spying on the panzers and the armoured men, safe as birds, Henryk with his little red train tucked under his armpit. But I was afraid. A shot in the head would take Mama from me forever. They would drag her back as Papa had dragged dead meat back from the forest. I stayed in the barn talking to my grandparents. I ripped the linen from the paintings and propped them up.

'Grandpa, what should I do? Will they come back? Will Papa come back? Are we going to hell?'

Grandpa, with the manor dangling on the horizon behind him. It was so still in the canvas. That was how I wanted it to be.

Jozef came back alone. He burst through the barn door, swollen and sweating and red. His fingers gripped the doorframe.

He took a breath before he spoke.

'They've taken them,' he said, panting.

He took his hand from the doorframe and wiped the sweat from his moustache.

'They were there already, you see. The pigs.'

He wiped his palm over his brow.

'And they would not let them go.'

His wife came up behind him and called me down. I did not speak. I turned back to my grandfather as Jozef climbed the ladder behind me and put his big hand on my head. I looked up into his donkey eyes and asked him would he take me back. He hid his eyes from me and turned away, back down the ladder.

'Stanislav, do you want them to take us all?'

'Why didn't they take you?' I asked.

'I was waiting for them in a field by the road. One of the farmhands told me that he'd seen everything. Big black car parked outside the front door. Those pigs inside looting like filthy Tartars. Their filthy flags hanging all over the house. Your Mama saw it all but she went in anyway. And she's a proud woman. Nothing would stop her. I swear to the Good Lord I could smell that danger from the field. It is the smell of evil, Stanislav. It has the stench of evil. I don't know Germans but I know them now. There's no mercy in them. You'll have to stay here with us.'

The smell of baking bread, and Jozef's sweat. I could not smell the evil, as Jozef did.

I shouldn't blame Henryk: I should blame the Germans and the Russians. But it is easier to blame the little boy who sulked for his red train when the Germans were invading. We had some time left, but Henry ruined everything.

I remember when butterflies would visit us in the nursery. Henryk would follow them around, clumping his feet on the floor in a ritual of adoration. He said that he would be a pilot. Papa could not suffer this spoilt, effeminate boy, this *idiot* that wanted to fly like the butterflies. For days before his conscription, Henryk hung about him like a deranged, overgrown insect, begging to fly with Papa.

'I am not going to fly, Henryk. I am going to fight. For Poland.'

One night in 1939, Papa left Lvov on a chestnut horse for the Hungarian border, where he was to join up with the Polish Army. He had joined the RAF Polish Squadron 303 in London. Later he died in the Battle of Britain. Or so we thought. Some grim reaper told Mama a different story later on.

3

Jozef tended to his potatoes. I watched him through the window. His huge hands ripped into the earth and sweat dribbled down his back. The sky was endless above him. Yes, I suppose he thought I would be eating that fodder in the winter.

That evening a Home Army soldier came to collect Mama, Henryk and me for the Kraków train. His name was Tomasz. Jozef bundled in out of the garden with earth caked on his hands, and told him, with his spade held across his chest, that no one would be going on the train to Kraków that night. Jozef shook his hand at me and told me not to say a word. A little piece of dry earth went into my eye. He held out his spade on the floor like a rifle and looked at me. My eye began to water. The grit scratched at my eyeball. I would eat potatoes through the vicious winter. I would give my hands to the earth and dig with Jozef. They would turn me into a peasant boy and they would take my books. The Germans would come, one day before the war was over, and they would shoot us to death in the barn.

Late that night, when the panzers were asleep, there was a knock on the door. A peasant crept in. His eyes were everywhere at once: he had adapted well to war, the little ferret. Jozef knew him; his name was Vladimir. He was barefoot, and wore a frayed straw hat on his head.

He greeted us in Ukrainian. He leaned forward and spread his fat brown fingers on the table. I saw swollen veins throbbing under his skin.

'I has news.' He rummaged in his pocket and opened up a folded piece of paper.

'I has it here.' He smirked. He handed it to Jozef, who opened it, glanced at it and handed it to Tomasz.

'You must read it,' Jozef told him. I saw: it was Mama's handwriting.

'Stanislav Malinski, you will go to your mother's sister in Kraków. Magdalena Dobczowska, number three Saint Bronislav's Street. I will take you to the station.' Vladimir gave me a sly half smile. Jozef turned toward the windows and looked out at his potatoes.

I was leaving. I possessed almost nothing of my own. I fled to the barn to find Papa's rococo clock. I grabbed it and wrapped it in a cloth. I pressed its hands back onto its enamel face, hoping for one moment that I could stop time and this whole infernal mess. I looked for grandpa, but he'd fallen over. I looked out at the sky through a hole in the barn wall: a stiff iron bird moved through the sky in a straight line. It roared and left a trail of smoke behind it. I took the clock and ran.

I left Lvov under a blue sky. German soldiers patrolled the station and glared at passers-by. There was a black spider on the flag they'd hoisted over the railway station. It cracked like a whip in the wind. I saw an old man with a beard, limping along with a battered case. A yellow star was pinned to the arm of his coat. I saw his hungry, sad eyes. He looked at me and I was sure I knew him from somewhere—was he some old friend of Papa's? I did not remember seeing such a bedraggled old man in our house. I did not remember those gloomy eyes. But I was sure I remembered something of him.

We heard a sudden 'Halt!' behind us. We turned around. I saw a soldier spit words at the old man, I saw him prod the old man's chest with his stiff hand. The old man dropped his eyes to the soldier's polished boots, and the soldier led him away. The old man and his yellow star disappeared into the back of a lorry. Gone. I was sorry for him but glad I did not have to get into the lorry with him. I was glad to leave him behind, even if Papa had once known him.

I turned to Tomasz. He was a slim man with a slim nose. I've just remembered that. Sweat shone on his cheeks and forehead. His lower lids were inflamed; his eyes looked sore. There were tiny crumbs of sleep nestling in his eyeducts. Tomasz did not look at the foreign eyes that looked at us. He knew better. Before we left, he had packed my father's rococo clock into a small suitcase. I clung to it as if it were the last piece of time left in the world. Then I began to think of Kraków: the poppyseed cake Aunt Magdalena would offer me from her three-tiered cakestand. That would be nice. Perhaps Kraków wouldn't be so bad after all. But then I wondered if they had confiscated her silver and all her cake. Could they take her cake? I imagined my Aunt Magdalena, stretched out on her chaise longue, pinched and pale from hunger, with missiles and grenades singing past her window. I asked Tomasz about poppyseed cake, in the most underground voice I could muster.

'No more cake for your aunt. Do you know what a calorie is? The Germans have an allowance of 2,613 calories a day. The Poles have 669. That means if they get three potatoes you get a pea. Don't tell anyone you know that. Let it be your first taste of manslaughter. Hope your aunt has a vegetable patch.' He did not look at me as he said it. He blew it, sideways, out of his closed mouth. I thought he was a little mean. I was glad he would not be travelling with me to Kraków. He did not know my aunt's resourcefulness.

'Have you been to Kraków lately, sir?'

'No.'

'Can I still go to the cinema there? Aunt Magdalena brought us there the last time. We saw—'

'Keep your head down and keep quiet. One of those devils is coming towards us.'

A woman came towards us. She had bulbous calves and broad shoulders. She had brown hair with the front pieces tied back. She had green eyes, an angular nose and a small mouth with a pronounced cupid's bow. I thought she looked nice. I smiled at her. She stared at us and did not return the smile. The tune of *Für Elise* kept playing in my mind, and this warmed me to her.

'Sir,' I whispered, 'is she a soldieress?'

'Can't you see her bloody uniform? Don't say another thing. Don't say anything. I'll deal with this.' She stopped in front of us. I remember that. She did not look so old—younger than Mama,

I thought. Like a big schoolgirl. I was not scared of her. I thought she had no reason to hate me. *Für Elise* played on. A bony hand on yellowed keys: our piano in the manor.

'Papers. Giff me your papers.'

Tomasz gave them to her, and he hid his tremble.

'Where are you going?' She had a thin gap between her teeth.

'The boy is going to Kraków.'

'Krakau? Ze train is late. One hour. Do not loiter. Do not drink.'

And she turned and left, her thighs trapped under her army skirt.

'That was the bitch that confiscated my cousin's sheep. They'll be having a feast up in your house, boy. Roast rack of lamb and sauerkraut and your poor Mama locked in the attic with a raw potato. You're lucky you escaped, boy. Your own house is the district SS HQ. You're damned lucky. Someone's looking after you.'

4

Today I will go shopping. I will buy some pork and cabbage. I do not like carrots or turnips or parsnips or beets. I don't even like potatoes. They breed in bad earth. I fear what poison those tubers and roots have soaked up down there. But of course I am as contaminated as they are. I open my window in the morning and look up at the sun, if it is there, and fill my lungs with sweet sulphur dioxide. And Mama's pickles, have they turned to poison? I should eat them. Good, wholesome, fifty-year-old gherkins and onions and beetroots, poisoned by history.

I will feed Henryk the pickled delights and a small cluster of pimples will settle over his brow as an insidious reminder of the war. I cannot forget. I will go shopping now. I will take a tram to the market. I will see the old people, older than myself, heave themselves onto the tram. How their heads droop and their eyes are cast down. They do not believe that a future exists. There is only the past. I have watched them grow old. Pay homage, pay homage. Remember this Remembrance Day, remember that Remembrance Day. It is illegal to forget.

The West has been allowed to forget. From what I understand, time moves very fast in western parts. Time is a precious commodity dealt out unwillingly by their technological contraptions. We should be thankful to the Russians, that they liberated us from time. How else could we remember so much, if we had not had that stretch of temporal sterility?

I have too much to remember. There is not enough room left in my mind for the future. There are others whose lives are shorter, who have less to remember. We old whiners, we spend the days dribbling out our cursed pasts, making the air heavy. The memory of our suffering hangs around them like a musty old coat that is not theirs. We wake up old ghosts. *We remember.* They should understand that it is impossible for us to forget.

I waited eight hours for the train to Kraków. Tomasz was silent. A silence that pitched us miles apart. Papa had told me about camaraderie in war. But I was nothing to Tomasz but a spoilt child of the gentry whose genteel mother was about to spill the underground beans.

I sat there like a mute, watching mothers weeping, soldiers walking up and down the platform. As I climbed up into the train, Tomasz squeezed my hand, and we parted. His hands were sweaty, like Mama's and Jozef's. Palms sweating in the war and the boom-boom echo of my heart inside the jacket of my bones. No one left now, no one left and would Aunt Magda have some cake? There, I left Lvov and I have never been back.

I nudged past the passengers on the train, my little case banging against their shins and knees. I found a seat between a man in glasses and a fat woman knitting a pair of socks. She smelt of oil and sweat and soap. A pair of socks, in the middle of the summer—for someone in Siberia? Who knows. Flies droned in the dead, warm air. The man in glasses put my suitcase on the rack.

'Thank you, sir.'

'You're welcome.'

'What time is it, sir?'

'I'm afraid I don't have a watch.'

War took watches from gentlemen, hats from ladies, cake from aunts, toy trains from little boys. That was what I thought, when the man in glasses told me he had no watch. I had always expected men in glasses to know the time.

Halfway to Kraków, the train was stopped and searched by SS guards for vodka. Thanks to Nazi obedience, my father's rococo clock survived. The officer's eyes gleamed a little when he opened up my case. But it would have been illogical to take it. 'Here, Sir, are sixteen bottles of illegally distilled vodka and a rococo clock' would not have appealed to the Nazi psychology.

5

Kraków frightened me. I walked, with my little case, up to the Main Square by Mariacki Cathedral. The last time I had seen it was before Henryk was born. It was Christmas time and the square was covered with a tablet of snow. People came out of Mariacki in procession. There were candles and accordions and men in hats. All this I saw from under Mama's coat, through blobs of quiet falling snow. Aunt Magdalena led the procession and laid a nativity scene under the statue of Adam Mickiewicz. Inside there, I heard Mama say, inside the statue, were the words of Adam's poems.

Now it was a stark summer day and there were soldiers marching, and the red-black banners of the New World hung from the windows of the square. An eagle eyed me from the Linen Hall. I sneaked away down Shevska Street. I wandered down the cobbled streets until I came to Wawel Castle. And there was the Black Spider on the red flag at the summit. I ran down the river to Salvator, where Aunt Magda lived. It was very quiet there on the tree-lined road. I saw shiny black cars sitting there, waiting for their drivers. Perched over the headlights were stiff little Nazi flags on silver poles. The Spidermen were staying on Aunt Magda's street.

My Aunt Magdalena was a better Catholic than my mother. A huge image of the Black Madonna hung in the hall beside the clock. The Madonna was everywhere; statues of her perched on shelves and windowsills and a white one over the bathroom sink, hanging from a nail that hooked into a hole in her back. A tall blue statue of her faced out onto the street.

Dark festoons hung under Aunt Magda's eyes. I could see the bones in her hands peeping through her skin. When she saw me, she put her hands on her hips and drew in a breath.

'There will not be much to eat. You know that, don't you?' I was sure she had hidden the poppyseed cake. I saw her silver three-tiered cakestand in the corner, pale and lustreless, waiting for the war to finish.

'There are rations. Do you know what rations are?'

I nodded, and set down my bag.

'They get three potatoes,' I said, 'and we get a pea.'

'Open your bag, boy. Have you brought anything?'

I opened it and showed her the clock. Its golden rays gleamed out at her. 'It is your father's clock?'

'Father's dead.'

'But the clock is not. We could sell it.'

She would trade my father's clock for bread. She snatched it out of my case and locked it away in one of her mouldy rooms. She told me, with an eyebrow arched, that without this sacrifice we might starve. It was my duty to God, and my attachment to it could lose me a seat in heaven. She said I was a dirty little atheist, and she made me read the passage about the seven candlesticks in the Book of Revelations seven times just so that I would know what was in store for me. As I read, she polished the brass arms of my clock with sickly globs of ammonia, the last of it we'd see before the war was over.

That night, I plotted my revenge. I feigned the suicide of a Virgin Mary, ten centimetres tall (the smallest, so it wouldn't be too big a sin). She flung herself from the sitting-room window and crashed on the pavement with an immaculate little tinkle. I was satisfied. In the morning my aunt dribbled out her Hail Marys, and I celebrated my alibi. For years Aunt Magdalena lived with the conviction that the statue had fallen to Germanic forces of evil.

In the morning, after she had swept the virgin chips from the road, my aunt marched into town with the clock. I watched the clouds cave in over each other. I wanted them to smuggle me away. I had nothing left. No Mama, no Papa, no Henryk, no time. It was as if I, as a character in some idyllic book, had been ripped out from the seams and transplanted into another, more sinister tale. I glanced around at the holy statues. Aunt Magda was not like she used to be. There was no cake, and she had forgotten to give me a present when I arrived. She stole my clock instead. What had the Spidermen done to her? Why was it so different, even here? I had no answer, so I wept and the holy statues stared.

My aunt came back with a scowl on her face. The antique dealers did not want the clock.

I watched her through the keyhole of my door. She paced the room, stopped to genuflect, paced again, then hurled herself to the floor and with a giant wooden set of rosary beads begged the Black Madonna of Czestochowa to resist the enemy. *Let them go home*, she said. *Let them go home. Like the Swedes, let them go home. God save our Poland, let us be free.* When she came out of the room she launched a tirade against the Jews.

'Filthy black communist Jews! They are the cause of our downfall, do you know it! Stanusz! Do you know it?!'

'Yes, Aunty.'

She stood over me in her blue dress.

'Oh, Stanusz. Little Stanislav. My little orphan. I will take care of you now. Little, little Stanusz.'

She leaned down and held me in her arms, muttering into my ears, *those filthy Jews, those filthy Nazis …*

'When will Mama and Henry come, Aunty?'

'They will come, Stanusz, when Poland is free. They will come.'

My aunt had been a regular customer at the antique shop for thirty years. A Jewish family had owned it. The clock, then, would stay with us. So I had my little piece of time, and every day I prayed in front of it that my Papa and my Mama would come back.

One day I asked her about the Jews. She rubbed her beads. She did not answer me. I asked again.

'What happens to the Jews in the ghettos, Aunty? Do they ever come out? Papa had Jewish friends.'

'That is why you have been sent to me. To be cleansed. I see it now. Come here, child.'

She pressed a crucifix to my forehead and forced me to repeat two hundred decades of the rosary. *Pray for Poland, Stasiu, pray for Poland*. Then she sank back into the chair with her arms hanging down and her pert mouth wide open. Angels sang divine verse through her windpipe and her nostrils. I decided I would venture into the night.

I walked along the walls of Wawel Castle. In the river the swans stared gormlessly at nothing. I stared gormlessly at them. I remembered the dragon that King Krak had killed under Wawel Castle. Was it not time for his Second Coming? He could swoop down from the night sky and bellow his flames over General Frank. With one whip of his tail he could fling the troops into the river. Why was there nothing to combat the evil that had descended on us? Could we not call upon this great force to save us? Where were the sorcerers when we needed them? Then I thought of my aunt. The dragon was only a dirty old pagan, she would have said. That was why they had killed him.

By the river I heard a rustle in the trees. Had somebody seen me? I looked back. There was something colourful in a tree. There was not much light left, but as I moved closer I saw a young man perched like a giant bird on the bough of the tree. He was painting. I, with a fearless dragon protecting me, asked him what he was doing.

'Painting, stupid.'

'Why?'

'Can't you see the moon? I am painting the seat of the Kings.'

'But—the soldiers.'

'They can't see me and if you shut up they won't hear me.'

'Can I come up the tree?'

'If you can climb. It's not my tree.'

I scrambled up the tree trunk and huddled on the branch beside him.

'How long have you been here?'

'Since the dark. I saw you looking at the river. You should be careful. I saw a man shot today for no reason at all. I saw all the professors being shoved into a big van and driven away to God knows where. They can take you away at any time if they want to. They decide. That's all.'

'Are the cinemas open?'

'Some are. But they only show stupid German films.'

'That's a good painting.'

'Wawel Chapel by moonlight. Spot the difference.'

'What do you mean?'

'Between the chapel dome in my painting and the chapel dome over there.'

I looked at his bony fingers hovering over the paper. He was a lean, sullen boy with puffy, elfin eyelids.

'Yours is gold and that's black.'

'Correct.'

'Why?'

'Because we covered it in tar before they came! Me and my father and his friends. We have ordained ourselves protectors of the Seat of the Kings. We will be famous heroes when the war is over.'

Then we heard laughter. A German officer staggered out from behind a bush with his jacket flapping open. He raised his bottle to the moon. He threw his head back, plunged it forward, and rammed the bottle into his mouth, dribbling rabidly, howling with joyless laughter. It relieved me to see the symmetry of a German shake and roar like that. His master was the vodka, his mistress the moon. The Führer did not fit into this at all. Then the searchlights pounced on him. In the middle of Wawel gardens, he swayed his arms above his head, surrendering his vodka to the law.

'Halt! Was machen sie?!'

'Ich trinke polnische Wodka, Herr Feldwebel. Heil Hitler! Hic!'

The sergeant marched over, beat him on the head with a baton, swiped the vodka, and dragged him home. My friend and I parted, and I made my way back.

I walked up Saint Bronislav's hill with the little wooden onion-towered church and the cemetery halfway up it. The moon hung to the left of the church; I fancied I could take it down and balance it on the steeple. Things did seem so mobile in the war.

I felt heroic, prowling around in a night of war. I walked home when the moon had disappeared behind a blanket of cloud. Instead of going upstairs I went downstairs to the dungeons of the building. I had seen my aunt go there and I wanted to know why. Cobwebs tickled my ears in the black dark. I felt my way to a door and swivelled open a rusty bolt. It creaked. I walked through and fell down a step and gashed my knee. There was a cold silence. I saw a crack of light at the end of the room. I fell over something metal that sighed like a gate opening and clattered to the floor. I came to the crack and pulled at a board. It came away easily. Moonlight poured in and all over the far wall were shelves of jars. I could just see them in the grainy light: plump gherkins, pearly onions, all swimming in brine. Silver rollmops and burgundy cherries. The labels read *July 1938*. These were Mama's jars. She had brought them here for Magdalena that year before the war.

I left them there, my inheritance. I went to my room. I lay on my bed and scratched my nose. It itched more. I scratched more. It itched more. I flung myself back on the bed. The itch began to spread. I itched and scratched like a flea-ridden dog. Some devil had sprinkled something on me in the cellar. One of Aunt Magdalena's enemies. I arched my back and kicked my legs. I swallowed my scream in the dark. I itched, scratched and drooled until I was raw and burnt. Then I slept and dreamt of Mama flying over Wawel on a little red train, waving to me in my little walnut boat. German tanks crept along the river like giant reptiles. Troops flanked the tanks, marching a mechanical drill. None of them saw Mama waving: they were like time itself marching mercilessly on, oblivious to the workings of the sky. I woke in the dark and flew to the window. But Mama had quit the sky.

6

How did a little red train merit such an epic rescue? Or did you, Mama, wish to melt the cold determination out of Henryk's eyes? You were too weak. Had he infected you with the fatal notion that mother and child could march in on a battalion of newly installed Nazis?

I see Mama clutching her little boy's hand, holding her hat down with the other, though there is no wind. She nears the manor that waits for her as patiently as it had done on her wedding day. There are banners draped all over her beloved home. It is the eagle on the banner hanging over the portal that spies her first. I see a panzer creeping up behind her, rolling over the barley in a vicious, arrogant advance. They had waited for the wet spring to come under the sun's command, for our crops to sprout, so that our annihilation could enjoy a pleasant backdrop. But they would perish in the winter, curled up in ditches under paddings of blue-white snow. Poor little Germans forgot that they could feel the cold. In spring we would find their bones where they had left them.

I see Mama rapping on the door—or does she pull the bell? Henryk is clutching at her skirt. I see sweat shining on her brow, dribbling down the bridge of her nose under the straw hat that shades her from the roasting sun. The fields are parched. The sun should have fallen out of the sky and shattered like a flimsy bulb in some quiet corner of the world. To show respect. Those diabolic armies did not deserve the light. They deserved a great black cloud to hover over them and deliver relentless rain and hail. The rivers should have swelled and dislodged the earth under their vicious boots. There I go again! My fantastic hatred.

And they got a petrifying winter, did they not? But I was speaking for Mama, putting myself in her canvas shoes in the July of 1941. I'm sure she hated the sun that day.

One night a peasant called to our door. He was selling vegetables. How cold it was, that Christmas. I remember Aunt Magdalena taking frozen beets off the cart, her bony fingers turning blue. She lay them out by the stove.

'Stanusz, this is our Christmas feast. Five beetroots and an armful of potatoes.'

'There's no carp?'

'The river has frozen over, Stanislav, and don't you know those devils would get them first?'

'There's no goose?'

'There's no goose. Help me, Stanusz. Help me peel these. My hands are frozen to the bone.'

Where was Mama now? Did she have carp? Did she have goose? Did Henryk? Did that little bastard have goose and carp? Were they in the manor still? Christmas, 1942. I pictured them there, beneath a candlelit Tannenbaum, surrounded by happy blond *kinder*, all of them singing *Stille Nacht* and sinking their pearly-white teeth into star-shaped German cookies. But I could not picture myself there.

I came back to the beetroots. It would be borsch for our Christmas Eve meal, and a few boiled potatoes. Aunt Magdalena handed me a jar of Mama's pickles, to cap our feast. I heard voices below on the street. Germans. Their staccato tones fell on my ears like little pellets. I stayed at the sill and watched them in their stiff breeches, pummelling forward in rhythm with their speech. No one was on the street except those two soldiers. The real people were hidden away in dark rooms, peeping out at the dark New World as I was. That was what power was: keeping people behind walls while you marched about and chatted with the ease that you had stolen. I stayed at the sill, trembling a little, until the soldiers were out of sight.

7

One night they came to the house. It had become a habit of mine, to watch the men patrolling from the safety of my unlit sill. That night, there was a howling wind. It was the Eve of All Saints. The Day of the Dead. I think it was just before the Beetroot Christmas. Nobody dared approach the cemeteries with their flowers and their candles. And so we paid respect to our dead in the desolation of our homes. There were no processions from the monasteries to the graves, no droves of hatted ladies armed with cut chrysanthemums, no candles thickening the air with black smoke. Once, before the war, I had been in Kraków on this day. We had come to visit the grave of Mama's father in the cemetery on the hill near Kosciusko's mound. At night the candles would smoke your lungs but you could smell the shy fragrance of the flowers underneath. Women and men stood at gravesides with their heads bowed down, kneading their beads, praying into the long night of the dead. And the murmur of their prayers would haunt you. Thousands of candles burned to keep the souls alive, their flames glowing loyally, throwing shadows over the gravestones that stood so absolutely still.

On this occupied night, nobody visited the dead. The dead would walk anyway, would come to thank us for the flowers lain and the candles lit in all the years before. I am sure they came to visit because we could not visit them. That small wind slithering through the broken window brushed against us like a presence. But the walls stayed obstinately quiet. Then the doors slammed downstairs in the bowels of the building.

'What is that?'

My aunt looked up from her psalm book, marked the page with the red ribbon, stood and placed it on her cushion.

'Germans! I can hear them!'

Their boots hit the steps like hands applauding our doom. Up they marched, up and up, and we had no time but the time between us and those boots, and we had no space but the box where we were trapped. We waited for the night of the dead to end. The statues spoke to me: they said we didn't stand a chance, that they'd been fooling my old aunt for a long time now. This was the end. The boots came closer, and the virgins did not move. I clutched Aunt Magdalena's hand but she threw it off. The herd of boots arrived. The knock on the door came then. *Tat-tat-tat. Tat-a-tat-tat.* My aunt rattled towards the door. As she turned the last key the door flew open and the troop poured in. The enemy was in our home. I had never come so close to one of these: seven of them, so awfully tall, in stiff black leather trench coats and green helmets. I admired them for this beautiful, strident power they had. Every gesture threatened attack. The smallest soldier took a handkerchief from his pocket to wipe his nose, and his black leather coat gave out little groans. They stared at the stricken room. The eyes of the tall officer pounced upon my aunt.

'You.'

His eyes shot down to her feet and up to her head with steel authority. My aunt said nothing.

'You are Magdalena Dobczowska, yes?'

'Yes.'

My throat felt hot, as if someone already had their fist around me. The clock ticked on, ignoring our plight.

'We have orders from SS High Commander Ruchenburg to search this house for Jews. Any Jews found on the premises will be shot to death. Anyone discovered hiding Jews will be shot to death.'

The statement required no answer. Ruchenburg, who sat with General Frank on the stolen Seat of the Kings in Wawel Castle, required no answer. He required dead Jews. The officer turned swiftly to his men and gave his orders. They dispersed and set about their search. One of the officers, with rosy podgy cheeks and a friendly potbelly, stood in the corner by the door. Surely this was all an inconvenience—this Jew-hunting, this fighting—so far from the homely custom of beer-drinking, song and roasting meat? He was a Santa Claus, miscast, in black. So far from home! Surely it was Ruchenburg who had put him up to this, who had forced him out of his dear old lederhosen?

Aunt Magdalena dropped her face into her handkerchief, and swore to them she had never let a Jew into her house. Hunched beneath the officer, she began to shrink.

'And he, who is that?'

'My nephew.'

'His name?'

'Malinski, Stanislav.'

'His papers?'

'Certainly.'

'Yours?'

'Of course.'

She scuttled over to her cabinet, pulled the documents out of a secret drawer and handed them to the officer. He snatched them from her and gobbled up the information.

'He came from Lvov?'

'Yes.'

'Why is he here?'

'He—had nowhere else to go.'

'His parents?'

'They are dead.'

'Dead. Who killed them?'

He barked out a laugh that saved her from answering.

'Maybe they are in a work camp?'

'No, sir.'

'Maybe they are dead. Maybe they are alive. Living or dead, it is no concern of mine. What is my concern is that they might be Jewish.'

'I assure you, sir, they were not. So the boy is not. Not a trace of Jewish blood. I assure you.'

'We shall see! There is a large Jewish population in the city of Lemberg. Do not think I do not already know that. And the boy has dark eyes. I shall see for myself is he a filthy little Semite or not. Schmutzig Judenhund, 'raus!'

He strode toward me. His hand, flat on my chest, forced me back onto the chaise longue. His other hand undid my trousers. The lower lip glistened, the eyes were bloodshot, the breath carried with it a syrupy smell of alcohol. A faint whistle came through his finely chiselled nose. He glanced down at my uncircumcised organ and shame flashed across his face, then disappeared again beneath his writhing hate.

'Hah! No Jewboy! Das ist kein Jude.'

He turned back to my aunt.

'You are under suspicion of unlawfully concealing a Jew in this building. Sixteen Jews have escaped from the ghetto in Podgorze. One of them was Chaim Bernstein, an antique dealer from the Kazimierz district. You were a frequent customer at his antique shop.'

'I never—'

'Silence, woman!'

He brushed away the dust from his stiff black coat.

'Your name is recorded in the accounts book of that antique shop. With no further discussion, we shall assume that you were acquainted with the Jew. You were on close terms. You purchased many valuables from the Jew. We have the evidence. Now, where is he?'

My aunt stared beyond the officer and rested her eyes on the Black Madonna icon beside his right ear. She stood up straight, and clasped her hands behind her back. She stared the officer in the eye, and spoke.

'I had business with the Jew in question. But I was not on friendly terms. I am a Catholic and do not mix with that sort.'

Out of the silence came the sound of a woman wailing. A howl of eastern prayer followed. Metal rattled. There was a final scream that jarred first, then faded and ended with the sound of crashing metal and a soft, human thud. The officer leaned out of the open window. He guffawed. Women, below, began screaming. There was gunshot. The officer glared at us as he summoned his soldiers from their futile search.

'That old Jew bitch was thrown out of a window on a wheelchair! I told you there were Jews in the building—did you not know?! Are you happy now, you Polish Catholic vermin—happy now the Jew is dead? Ja?'

Then our rosy-cheeked officer left, and his six disciples followed. I never saw him again and I will never forget him. Sometimes, in the pit, his shadow passes over me.

8

I think I shall have some tea to clear my mind. I will go to the centre and find Jan. He will drink tea with me. Jan and I used to lecture together in the faculty of architecture. We used to drink vodka together. Now we drink tea. Jan has a very large nose and was nearly thrown out of the faculty for it in the purges of '68. He managed to prove to the authorities that God had made his nose that way, and not the Jews. He kept his job. I, however, did not. But I will speak of that later.

Henryk will come in a week—is it a week now? He will come and he will see me slumping at the edges of my life, and he will see the shadows and the yellow swans and he will choke in the sweet sulphur dioxide. He will leave again, and he will never come back. He will desert me as he deserted me before.

How to be free? Should I jump from my window and dive into the gritted air? I need to know. Perhaps Henryk will know.

I shall not go for tea with Jan. He will say I'm sulking and morose. He doesn't understand. And yet why should he understand? Why should he be dragged into my pit? It is not so desirable a place. Jan is just two years my junior, but he doesn't dwell on things. He moves in relatively straight lines. He lost both parents and a sister in the Warsaw Rising. But he does not look back. He does not rummage, as I do. He says I am the only man he knows who is nostalgic about the war. I find this mockery offensive, but I like him still. He is a cheery man. He is defiantly happy. Happy about everything except his nose. It has caused him a lot of trouble in his time and he has no idea where it came from. Neither of his parents possessed such a crooked, angular thing. He does not know if he got it from his grandparents, since his family albums were destroyed in the pyre that consumed his parents. Intimately, he has told me his secret theory on the matter: that it had grown in sympathy with the Jews. And there was not a trace of mockery or anti-Semitism in what he said. His parents had some very close friends in the Warsaw ghetto, and so, I suppose, did he.

That lymph node is beginning to bother me. Every time I lean back into my armchair I feel it there. The little growth cannot take the pressure, positioned, as it is, on the back of my head. I will have to have this seen to before Henryk comes. And what about my ochre-grey face, my missing teeth, the tightening sinew that is disabling my hand? My nylon clothes. My imitation leather shoes. What will Henryk think? He will view me with distaste. He will not want this shabby victim as a brother. I do not care.

I see the swan paddle toward the bridge. The river is as still as a sheet of glass and the sun is shining splendidly above it and everything looks well arranged today. I feel quite pleased. It was like that the day I heard the Russians had taken Lvov back from the Germans. My heart sank to the bottom of the river. I knew that Mama and Henryk would not come for me. I knew that I would never see Mama again, that she would fly away as Papa had. The glassy river stayed obstinately still. And the Red Army marched in.

That week, Stalin was welcomed like a friendly hero. I did not take part in the celebratory marches. By the time the Russians had garrisoned us in behind grey slabs, Mama had settled in the middle of a green island on the safe edges of Europe, as far away from Stalin as she could get. She went to Ireland. How she got there, I do not really know. I shall have to ask Henryk.

One day, after the war, a letter arrived from Ireland. A clean, white tiding from the West, sitting in the bottom of our rusty post-box. On a Tuesday or a Wednesday. *My Stanislav, my love, come and join your mother. Little Henry misses you and I am crying as I write.*

She told me too much. The coloured patchwork valleys. The sweet damp rain. The friendly people. The nightmare over. How her soul sang. And what was I to do? To write to her of Stalin? To tell her the shops were empty, that I had had to wear a Nazi uniform to keep me warm in the winter of 1946? To tell her her sister had well and truly lost her mind? How could I throw my dark shadow over her brand new solace, when she'd lost so much? But so had I. It wasn't fair. War had done this. But I could only blame her, and Henryk.

They got their paradise. When they arrived in Ireland, a family took them in. Every refugee's dream. Mama and Henryk stayed with them for some months while they helped Mama find work. It was as if she was a relative of theirs, and not some wretched Polish refugee. It was as if a large grey animal had sat down between Mama and me, and it refused to move. She had abandoned me for the purples, greens and saffrons of another land. Colour had fled from my life and I could see no sign of it returning. I choked on the invisible Soviet poison that claimed our air. Back there: the air was so clear it sang, the grass was a green shawl, the moss soft velvet, the people garrulous, warm and well fed. They ate buxom cows from the fields and drank thick black beer. They drank many pots of tea in a day. Mama had the impression that these people talked a lot—or was it just that she had not had a conversation in three years? No, she was not mistaken. They talked a lot. In fact, there were no silences at all.

Why did Mama have to grind it in like that? Why did she write to me of her heavenly refuge, knowing I'd been left in hell? Mama's letters never referred to the war. Occasionally she would refer to her 'shame', her 'guilt' and her 'pain'. But the war was a pit she had climbed out of. Her letters became foolish, self-deceptive little sermons on the bright flowers and the pleasant weather and other such insipid joys.

But one day, she wrote to me of Papa. She told me a thin, yellow man in knee-high black boots and a long black coat came to the hotel where she was working. He had a terrible cough and he said in Polish that he would soon be dead. He had TB. He was one of RAF Squadron 303: he had known Papa.

Between his coughing fits, in the calm, he sighed. To Mama he was as unwelcome as any grim reaper. He had come, Mama told me, to tell her that there was no hope. Papa was most definitely dead. Flying Officer Ryszard Kuron had seen him clutch his heart and grope for breath as a fish bone speared his gut outside a fish and chip restaurant in Belfast. Flying Officer Kuron saw to it that he got a decent burial. He put him in a field outside the city. He could take Mama there if she wished, or at least give her directions, since his health might not allow it, and death might come at any moment …

Flying Officer Kuron took her to Belfast on the Sunday train. They found the plot on Monday morning. She covered the plot in flowers, lit some candles and took the train back to Dublin.

She could not believe that her husband was buried there in the field, in the north of this little island that before the war she had hardly heard of. Now she sat on this land, walked on it, ran on it, worked on it, breathed in it. But no matter how she tried she could not believe her husband was buried in it. She tried to contact Flying Officer Kuron, but he had already died, swallowed up into another grave. There was only one thing she could do to set her mind at rest. She would have to go back up to Belfast and dig her husband out.

She bought a spade and set out towards the grave. There lay her wilted brown flowers. The makeshift cross still stood. She began to dig. She was not very good at it, but she persevered. Poor Mama. How strange she must have looked: a fair, slim woman ripping into the earth with a big thick workman's spade. Poor Mama. What a search. The worst of it was that she found him. His bones, shrouded by his gobbled tattered uniform. Nothing left of Papa but his bones and his wedding ring and a rotted uniform. No smile around his teeth, no eyes in his sockets. Only the white bones that keep us all together. ... Those years they spent together in the manor, with music and hunting and meals at the long table and the children that grew between them and the seasons behind them, in the manor, on the veranda, in the orchards, golden, the sun setting, rising, setting, rising—it all came to this. A woman in a grey coat staring at the bones of her husband in this damp, hostile piece of earth on an unknown island. She prayed for his soul, grabbed the finger bone with his wedding ring on it, and left.

I choked on my tears for Papa, and dreamed of this foul image for weeks. I came to the grave and held out my hand where Papa lay intact as if in a bed of earth. When he rose out of the grave he leaned down to kiss my head and when I looked up at him he had turned to bone and I stared into his empty sockets. There was too much death. I pitied Mama but I still raged. I might have been a stack of bones to her. I was as good as dead.

9

Hunting for Colorado Beetles in the grass. Comrade Stalin said the CIA had dropped them from the air. It was a conspiracy to destroy our crops, they said. I remember that madly sunny day. We filed onto the bus, delighted to be missing Thursday's history class. That was the day I recognized Roman. He was one of the older boys. He had spindly fingers and knobbly, scabby knees. Those were the spindly fingers that sketched Wawel Chapel on a moonlit night in the war. He scowled at me. His knuckles tightened around the seat rail.

'Do you remember me?' I asked him.

'Yes, stupid.' He looked out the window, away from me.

'Did your father take the tar off the chapel dome after the Nazis left?'

'No, stupid. He's an Enemy of the People. He's in prison.'

'So you never saw the chapel gold? You never got your medals?'

'No, stupid.'

'And your relations?'

Roman turned around and faced me.

'Enemies of the People. All in prison. Why do you think we're looking for beetles that don't exist? *We are all in prison.* STALIN IS A DESPOT!'

Everybody heard. The supervisor called him over. Roman clenched his teeth, and blushed.

His body held no conviction: it was a stooping, gangly thing. He was led away by the supervisor, out of the bus. He would be sent to some reformatory school or to the army. I see him as our country was then: spindly, gangly, bitter—not fit to fight the second enemy.

I remember my twelfth birthday. Bitter cold. I had hoped for something from the West: a giant parcel of chocolate, coloured pencils, toys. That would have had Aunt Magdalena prosecuted by the authorities, of course. Nothing came. Nothing but the vicious cold and the shocked silence that followed the war. Like a giant invisible bruise.

Aunt Magdalena had taken a bad turn. One day in 1944 she had flung her sparrow's body to the floor and wept until I could no longer see her eyes, they were so swollen. I had learnt to predict these fits. I could hear them approaching. Her breath quickened. She spilled out of her chair onto the floor, her fingers gripping her ears and her face smeared all over the carpet. It was awful to see. I could not bear it on my birthday. So I went out for a walk and left her, her beads clicking away in her old hands.

I went to the river under Wawel. It had frozen into a road of ice. The children were skating on it, tearing around the ice in circles, falling and laughing. My twelfth birthday. I thought I should tell them, but I had no skates. I sat on a rock at the riverbank and watched.

'Stanislav! Stanislav!'

A girl in a grey coat skated toward me.

'Hello,' I said.

'Stanislav! It's me, Anna. Anna Goralska. Don't you recognize me?'

Through the blue scarf I saw a sprig of light brown hair, and green eyes. Anna Goralska. She was very pretty but she couldn't remember dates in history. She sat in the desk behind me on Thursday afternoons. I looked at her: her hands in a muff, her skinny legs on blades. Then I saw her eyes. There were no nightmares in her eyes. She looked away and slipped then. I helped her up and she sat on a rock beside me.

'Here, have my muff, Stanislav. Are you cold?'

'No,' I said. I looked into her eyes again: Wawel Castle, and the sky. No nightmares in them.

'Do you not skate, Stanislav?'

'I have no skates. You skate very well.'

My voice did not seem to come from me, but from somewhere in the ice between us.

'I'm a ballerina,' she said, as if that was the answer. 'Why do you have no skates?'

'It's my birthday,' I said, as if that was the answer.

'Oh, Stanislav! Come to our house and have sausages! We have sausages and Papa will let you come because it's your birthday. Will you come?'

'Where do you live?'

'Chopin Street. Will you come?'

We went to Chopin Street. She brought me to a room with cracked panes in the window. Papa did not look up from his papers when we came in. There was a smell of dead tobacco and old cabbage. Mama was nowhere: the war had taken her. A bearskin lay on the floor. Jozef Stalin rested on a shelf in a plain wooden frame, and the Virgin Mary was nowhere to be seen.

'Papa! Papa! Stanislav is in my history class and it's his birthday. Can he have some sausage? He's so cold.'

'Sausage?' said Mr Goralski, lighting a cigarette.

'The sausage, Papa. You said …'

'Anna, Aniu. Do you know … that I have eaten it? Will you forgive your Papa? He ate it like a bear while you were skating. Papas get so hungry.'

Anna's fresh ice face went mottled, and withdrew. I had forgotten that daughters had fathers. She looked at me and shrugged.

'No sausage.'

Papa heaved himself up from the chair. He wheezed.

'Hello, Stanislav,' he said. 'How is your aunt?'

'Very well, thank you,' I lied.

'Anna says it is your birthday. Will you have some tea?'

He pulled on his cigarette. His fingernails were brown. We drank tea in the quiet, motherless kitchen while the Vienna clock ticked in the corner. There were no biscuits, and no cake.

'Heard from your mother, Stanislav?' He put a plate of stale bread in front of me. 'Eat it, you need it.'

'Mother writes,' I said, fingering the bread.

'Is she coming back? Is your sister coming back?' said Anna.

'No. Brother, not sister,' I said, and I dipped a corner of bread into my tea.

'What is she doing there? Why did she leave Poland? Seems to me … a little strange,' said Papa.

'I don't know,' I said, and I looked across the room at the picture of Stalin. A piece of bread was stuck in my throat. There was a photograph of Anna's mother beside Stalin on the shelf. Her name was Galina. She was in a Juliet costume, poised in three-quarter profile. Her lips looked black and her face was like plaster of Paris. Papa sat there puffing his sweet Chinese cigarettes, direct from Chungking. One eye gleamed at me through a cloud of smoke.

[43]

'War is a terrible thing,' he said. 'One fifth of our population gone. Warsaw a pile of dust. Communism is our last hope.'

'Yes,' I said. I thought of Mama and Henryk in their green valley, laughing over tea. Papa got up and crossed the room. He took Galina down off the shelf and put her on the kitchen table. Anna did not speak. It must be some old ritual, I thought.

'Anna is a dancer, like her mother. It is Anna's duty to dance, Stanislav. Galina danced for the Tsar in Leningrad. Anna will dance for Stalin. That is my wish. And you, Stanislav, what will you do?'

'I will build,' I said. It was something to say.

'That's my boy! That's what you'll do! Everybody must do something, that's the truth. Anna will dance, and you will build. Everyone will be happy. War is a terrible thing, but we will be happy again. Everyone will be happy.' He took Galina away and sank into his armchair by the stove.

10

It did not take Mama long to marry again. The man's name was Foley. Edward Foley. He was a columnist for one of Ireland's national newspapers. They lived in a house in the countryside, not too far from the family that had taken her in. On the same purple, green and yellow-flanked road.

Hodgkin's disease had taken his first wife. He had a daughter by the unpronounceable name of Siobhán. I suppose she replaced me adequately. Mama's God competently replaced all that she had lost: a husband, and child and a manor, of sorts. Pah! I bet they had an army of servants and a fowl-filled forest. I bet they had a television and a car.

She did not describe the house to me, though I did ask her to. So I am left with the image of a manor home, similar to our own, set against a patchwork valley of yellows, purples and greens. Nothing could dispel the image of this proud, spiteful manor from my mind. Amber light poured from her long windows, the front doors hung open, knowing I could never enter.

I am in the room, pressing my ear against the bureau. With my eyes closed now, I see Papa sitting here, scratching out his accounts with a thick nib. He sips a cup of Turkish coffee and presses his lips together. Mama moves up behind him and presses his shoulder lightly. His free hand joins hers. He does not turn around. He continues to scratch out these endless figures. As his arm moves across the desk, the hinges squeak. Mama leans down and her hair brushes against his. She rests her other hand on his free shoulder. She whispers into his ear. She has told him. The Germans have invaded Poland. The war has begun.

I asked Mama why he flew away but she did not tell me. I asked her again and again. But she would write to tell about Irish Catholics, Henryk's school, the rain. I do not know how long Papa was in the army and I do not know when he trained as a pilot. He was one of eighty Polish pilots who fought in the Battle of Britain. My Home Army cousin gave me a photograph of Papa, hunched with three other men beside a Spitfire with the letters RAF painted under its cockpit. Two of these men are holding a segment of a German aircraft with the words 'The 178th German Aircraft Destroyed by 303 POLISH (F) SQDN' painted in English over the swastika. Papa has that same grin on his face that he used to bring back from the forest when he'd captured something large and wild.

That image of Papa writing seems to persist, but only because Mama was there and only because of what she said. I remember Papa's hand moving across the page. He lit a cigarette after she'd told him. The smoke mingled with their fear of the enemy. That is all I remember. That was the only warning I got of what was to come.

I see the swans outside. Their reflections are dull on the dirty water. They do not know the filth in which they swim. They will die of it, without knowing.

Mama wrote to me over the years, and I rarely wrote to her. Is that sinful of me? She would not answer my questions, so I stopped asking them. But she asked questions. They were meaningless questions for which I could have given a few meaningless answers. She asked about my school and if I was eating properly. She asked if I passed my exams and how I liked university and if I did not think I should move out of my dead aunt's apartment. She asked if I found it cold in the Polish winters. She never mentioned Stalin.

Had Mama forgotten the white winters of Lvov? Our sledge like a winged Pegasus gliding over the ice, the spruce trees hanging low with snow, the lacework of the frozen birches. How could Mama forget that? What a romantic fool I am. That cold killed peasants. Immobilized us. Sterilized the earth. Steel winds assaulted us. People drank to shut out the cold. I saw Papa roar at staggering peasants in the middle of our winters. I saw frost in Papa's beard. Yes, I remember Papa with his frosted beard shouting at a red-nosed peasant and the forest undefined, beyond. I think I remember wolves howling but that might be from a story that I read. I remember one of Papa's Arabs skidding on the ice and falling on its belly. Steam puffed out of his nostrils. He was a chestnut.

I related these memories to Mama. My snow stories. She did not write back for some time. When she did, she said she missed the tile stoves in Poland. She wrote a short treatise on the subject, outlining the efficiency of this method of heating. There was a terrible dampness in Ireland that made her bones creak.

She wrote again and again asking me to come. A voice in my lumber-room said: *you should go, you should go.* But Papa Goralski had got a hold of me. And so, of course, had his daughter. Anna had been enrolled in the Warsaw Ballet School: Papa was forcing her into her mother's pumps. During that time, I only saw her four times a year. As for me, he had it planned that I would study in the School of Architecture. I was to build, out of the rubble that our great cities had become. I used to scrabble around the streets, taking parts of the dismantled city home. I put bricks and mortar and skirting board and glass in my rucksack and trekked up St Bronislav's hill, like Sisyphus. Ruined things: I wanted to make them new again. Yes, I was to build. I would never go to Ireland.

Papa Goralski dragged me out of Aunt Magda's dungeons. I joined the Union of Young Polish Socialists (ZSMP). I did it to please Papa, I suppose. Papa was an engineer. He was working on Nowa Huta, the New Steelworks. It was built just west of the Old City. A hulking mass of concrete was erected in the name of Socialism. A Worker's Paradise. A cloning of all that was grey. Workers, no better than serfs, were incorporated into the New Kingdom of Steel. Nowa Huta. Papa used to go there every day, and come home wheezing in the evenings.

The Steelworks chimneys puffed out yellow clouds all day. Paint peeled away from the walls of our old buildings, the stones began to crumble. I began to choke. I took to staying indoors when the weather was mild and calm, smoking my way through decades of Papa Goralski's Chinese cigarettes. His protégé turned a little yellow at the edges.

When he took me up to Warsaw to see Anna dance in *La Sylphide*, she said to me, behind a theatre door, with a sable coat crouched over her, 'You look sick, Stanislav.' And I nearly died. The cold air encased me, would not even let me blush. I was yellow, and that was it. *Anna, please show me, please show your little yellow man a sign of love.* I seized her limpid hand as Papa turned to greet a comrade. I held a fish. Her eyes were on Papa all the time. (In case he should have turned around, and caught untimely love.) Papa called me over with a sweep of his broad paw. He didn't notice the limp fish in my hand.

'Come here,' he said, 'and meet this man.'

It was Janusz Weiss, jelly-jowled chairman of the Warsaw Union of Young Polish Socialists.

'Here's a young architect,' Papa told Mr Weiss, and Mr Weiss offered his hand to the jaundiced, pubescent architect.

'Young Poland,' said the chairman, 'our fledglings. We will build Warsaw again. And all of Poland.'

The rest of the street was rubble, and I longed to burrow in it like a mole. I did not want to build a new Poland. I wanted to rebuild the old. My manor home. My Mama. Just in that moment, in Anna's absence. Perhaps always, yes, always.

I had to sit beside Mr Weiss in the auditorium. He turned to me half way through *La Sylphide* with tears shaking in his scarlet lids. He dabbed them with his handkerchief. I looked at Anna poised in a teetering arabesque on the stage. I closed my eyes and pictured her in a red dress on May Day, but it didn't fit. My little white sylph had made a Communist man cry. I longed for her, but left the demolished city without her, in the cold.

II

I never wrote to Henryk, until now. He remained in my mind as that small, spoilt little boy who led my mother away from me for-ever. I would never have written to him, until now. He wrote to me a month ago, telling me of Mama's death. I could feel the motor of my hatred winding down. Perhaps my hatred would die with her. I was bitter, yes, for all those years, but proud that I had suffered. Proud that I had endured the years here without them. Proud that I suffered more than they could ever have suffered.

I found the letter in the post-box on my way back from a visit to Jan. The same post-box that Mama's letters were delivered to. Now there is a hole in the lid of it from rust. I took the letter to my room and sat at the bureau with a cup of coffee. It was not Mama's writing, but the stamp was the same: a strange little bull drawn out of spirals. The letter was not evenly sealed. He must have done it in a hurry after the funeral. Why did he wait until after the funeral to tell me? I could have gone. Someone could have paid for me, over there. Anyway, it was a short letter: he did-n't give away too much.

> *89 Waterloo Road*
> *Dublin 4*

7 August 1990

Dear Stanislav,
This is your brother, Henry Foley. I hope that you are in good health. I'm afraid I carry bad news. Our mother died last week of a stroke. She'd had the first one just a month before this one took her. We had a funeral for her in the local church. We were sorry, of course, that you couldn't be there.

She did say, just before she died, that she wanted to see you. Now that is not possible, I would like to meet you. I would like to plan a trip to Cracow. Our mother's passing away has put a different perspective on things. I understand that you will need time to think about this, so I shall wait patiently for your reply before I make any preparations. I shall of course respect whatever decision you make.

> *Yours Sincerely,*
> *Henry Foley*

P.S. I would like to travel in the next month or two, if that is possible. Do you know if there are any cheap flights available?

Why do they speak English in that country? Is it not the greatest defeat, to have your own tongue defeated? I have heard they have a language that is incomprehensible to the English. Would they not speak it, proudly? Mama kept half his tongue Polish, I am sure. She could not have spoken to him in anything other than Polish. There would be no other way to speak intimately.

He says they're sorry I couldn't make it to the funeral. Who is *they*? Plural. Mama is dead. I know no one else but Henryk there. Does he expect me to acknowledge that man my mother married? Does he expect me to believe that *they* feel the pain that I feel? Mama is dead. My Mama. They took her from me and now she's gone forever. Henry Foley. Who is that? Why does he disguise himself? He is Henryk Malinski. If he is to be my brother, that is to be his name. Mama. I will go to the cemetery today and light another candle in her name. Mama.

But what does he mean by asking me about cheap flights? Does he think I am a seasoned traveller? Why does he ask me those questions? Does he do it to flaunt his freedom and his wealth? Who is this polite, reserved gentleman? I do not know him. I do not trust him. He is the little boy in disguise. He has come back to mock me.

No wonder I am yellow and grey. No wonder my teeth rot, my fingers seize up, my lymph node gathers fat. I cannot bear it. I feel so helpless and so stifled. Henryk will not understand all that we have been through. How privacy was banned, choice confiscated and luck abolished. How we waited. In queues that stretched from one end of the Main Square to the other. How one Easter hailstones the size of golf balls pelted down from the heavens as if God had collaborated with the Authorities. They bounced off the skulls of bent old ladies, young women, old men, children younger than I ever was. We were waiting for Good Friday's ham allowance. We held our papers, prayed there'd be enough. There could never be enough. The hailstones hit us hard.

A drunk came through the hailstones and stood beside a veteran of war. He had a furious red face. His nostrils flared. He had found a scapegoat.

'Hey old man! You're too old to eat ham! You'll be dead soon. Leave it for our kids.' The old man stared ahead.

'Fuck you, grandpa! I don't care about your fucking war! It was too long ago. What the hell did you fight for? Look at this queue! This is what you fought for!'

The old man turned away from him and pulled his beret right down over his ears. The hailstones lightened. We queued for another three hours.

Henryk will not believe that I spent half my life queuing. He will not believe that I only saw oranges at Christmas. Oranges from Cuba, blessed by Che Guevara. He will not believe that I have waited twenty years for a telephone. He will not believe it because they say it is all over now. Our stories seem tall to the West, I suppose. But won't my pallor tell him? Won't my thin body and my hunch tell him what they did to us? I'll tell Henryk, I'll tell him everything. I can't wait to see the expression on his face.

12

Papa Goralski had me enrolled in the Technical University. I was to be an architect. Anna stayed on in Warsaw but her visits back became more frequent. We had begun to kiss. And as soon as we did, Aunt Magdalena began to hate her. Anna was *a gypsy-jew, a filthy whore, a communist bitch.* She was the cause of the downfall of Poland. How she knew, I do not know. The Black Madonna must have told her.

One day I brought Anna home. Aunt Magda was staring out the window, clutching a cup of tea. She must have seen us coming. Young love, giggling under the trees: everything she never had. She had been kind to Anna, before this. She had fed her zurek soup and her favourite bread with caraway seeds. Anna and her father were our saviours, she had said. She too had encouraged me to build. Papa Goralski invited her to Chopin Street many times, but she always declined. 'I am a Pole,' she would say, 'I never leave my home.'

Anna stood in the hall by the Black Madonna, and I whispered to Aunt Magdalena that she had come.

'Get her out of my house, Stanislav.' That was all she said

then. She did not look away from the window. She just stared, and clutched her cup. Anna had not heard. I took her to the kitchen. She washed her hands in the sink with the white porcelain virgin hanging over it.

'Will she not talk to me, Stanislav?'

'You just stay here, Anna. I'll talk to her.'

But Aunt Magda said the same again: 'She must leave this house, Stanislav.'

'But Aunt Magda—'

'Get her out. She is a whore. She is a communist. She is destroying our home. You will fall, Stanislav. I see it: you will fall.'

I took Anna's hand and led her down the stairs, down the street, away from St Bronislav's Street. We walked to Kazimierz, the old Jewish district.

'What are we doing here, Stanusz? This place is full of thieves. What is wrong with your aunt?'

'She's mad.'

'Don't say it, Stanusz. She's your aunt.'

'She's mad. Now where can we kiss? Your Papa will smell our love on Chopin Street. We are exiles, Anna. So we must roam the streets of Kazimierz.'

'I can't. I don't like it here. It's full of drunks and thieves. Papa says it isn't safe.'

'Once it was full of Jews, you know.'

'Stanislav, I have to go. Papa is taking me to the train station. The Warsaw train leaves at six. I have to go: it's getting dark.'

'Anna, just come with me.'

She liked it when I said it like that. When I was like a ram, not a fish. I brought her to the Jewish Cemetery on Szeroka Street. There was nobody there. I pressed her against the cemetery wall. My knuckles scraped against the Hebrew inscriptions behind her back.

'Anna, Anna,' I said into her hair, 'you are my Anna.'

My hands moved over the lines of her body, over her hips and shoulders, down the spine of her back. And then, down between her legs.

'Don't, Stasiu. Don't. We're in a cemetery. We'll be cursed.'

'What do you care? It's Jewish.'

'Dead are dead. Jewish or Catholic. Stop it, Stanislav, stop!'

And she pushed me away.

'Don't you love me, Aniu? I brought you here because, because this is where King Kazimierz met with Esther, his Jewish lover. He built a tunnel from Wawel Castle just to—'

'That's nonsense, Stanislav. It's getting dark. Papa will be angry. I have to go, now bring me home.'

One week after that, Aunt Magdalena died. It was a modest resignation: reading her psalm book one spring evening, she sighed, let the book fall to her lap, and closed her eyes. They said it was a heart attack brought on by the changing air pressure of the *Halne* wind, but I knew she'd prayed for this. She had taken to dribbling as she hummed her prayers in the corner of her room, with the wind banging the window back and forth. I and the lady next door, a seasoned and dedicated funeral-goer, attended her departure to the earth. Anna came down from Warsaw, and Papa Goralski took the day off work. That was all. She was buried between a war memorial and the newly built cemetery wall. I sat by her grave in the warm spring evening, alone. I lit some candles and laid flowers between them on her grave. The new cemetery walls were quite imposing: like some cheap attempt to control death. So many people dead. I vowed, by my aunt's grave, to survive and live and build.

Mama sent me a package some weeks later. Full of lipsticks for Anna and medicines for me. I sold these treasures for food and coal. The penicillin fetched a nice price and I got 450 zlotys each for the lipsticks. My poor Ania thought our cemetery sin had caused Aunt Magda's sudden death. That a Jewish soul could have had anything to do with her death would have had my aunt turn livid. But Anna would not take my mother's lipsticks, and she refused to kiss in the house of a Dead Woman. For months, in some absurd respect for my aunt, we continued to kiss in Kazimierz.

One evening we sat under a tree in the old cemetery. There was a light rain falling, and it brought out a beautiful smell from Anna's skin. The smell of a fresh leaf, and flowers. I looked into her eyes, and there were no nightmares there. That was what I loved about Anna—she was the one thing in my life that had not been contaminated. So when she told me not to touch her there, I didn't. There we sat, King Kazimierz and Esther, under a birch tree in the cemetery.

'Anna,' I said, 'will you leave Warsaw?'

'No. I can't.' She turned to the cemetery wall.

'Why? Why do you have to dance? Is it your wish, or is it your father's? Who are you, Anna? Are you the shadow of your mother?'

'Stop it, Stanislav. Stop.'

'Do you love Warsaw, or do you love me?'

'I love you, Stasiu. You know I do.'

'Then leave! Leave Warsaw and come back to Kraków!'

'But Papa—'

'Papa?'

'Papa. I must dance. He'll be so hurt, if I don't dance.'

'Are you his slave?'

'Stanislav!'

'You are his slave! Daddy's girl—that's what you are!'

'You push me too far, Stanislav. Dancing is my life. That's all I have. All I have! I am not a slave, I am a dancer!' She ran out of the cemetery, away from me, down Szeroka Street and into a tram. Back to Chopin Street, back to her Master.

I took off down Szeroka Street and went home in the tram. That night, Aunt Magda's virgins were a comfort. I prayed to them my Anna would come back.

13

Stalin died in March 1953. It was my second year in college. In the lecture room, a pillar of sunlight slanted in over Stalin's faded portrait. Jan nudged me. He pointed to the window. Outside an irate peasant was whipping his dull old horse. He stamped his feet and cursed and shook his head. He heaved his whole body against the horse. He pushed him from behind with his head lodged between the horse's back legs. The horse took revenge. He relieved himself upon his master: large clods of steaming dung rolled down the peasant's back. He stood up with a burning red face and kicked the wretched horse in vain.

Jan hollered. He had forgotten what day it was. Our lecturer Mr Szymanski, a devoted Party member, shot round to find the culprit.

'Who has dared to laugh on this grave day?'

'I, sir.'

'You. You are no comrade of mine, Jan Pachocki. No comrade of mine. You dared to laugh on this grave day. Do you know who died today?'

'Yes, sir.'

'Who?! Who has died today? Tell me.' Spittle fired from his mouth and his glasses jumped down his nose. The peasant, outside, was still kicking the old horse.

'Jozef Stalin died today, sir.'

'Correct! And do you know what that means?'

'Yes, sir.'

'That means the great protector of the workers is no longer with us. That means thousands and thousands and thousands of workers will flock to their master's grave in Moscow and will mourn his death. As I do. As you should. But you laughed as if the day had not brought this terrible news. You laughed. Get out of my sight, Jan Pachocki. Go straight to the rector and tell him what you did.'

Outside, the peasant and his horse were trotting away down the street. The sun came out from under a cloud. Jan was sent to a reformatory school for seven weeks.

Our Father had died. Anna was in Warsaw; I believe she danced on the funeral day. I had not seen her since she stormed out of the cemetery. She had not written. I met Papa Goralski in the street one day.

'How is Anna, Mr Goralski?'

'She is dancing in Warsaw. She is very well. You can see her next week, she's coming down. Her legs are in pain, and she needs a rest.'

I came to Chopin Street the following Friday. Anna was pale and she had a limp. I sat down at the kitchen table. Papa's smoke sailed in, and I coughed. I coughed for five minutes.

'What's wrong with you, Stanislav?' she asked me.

'Laryngitis—it's the air here. I'm—choking.'

'Don't be silly, Stanislav. You're just ill.'

'No—it's the fumes. Nowa Huta—'

'Nonsense, Stanislav, it's the cigarettes! I should never have let you at them! Ha, ha!' Papa Goralski banged his fist on the arm of the chair. It was true: I smoked almost as much as he did, and I was only twenty.

'What a useless lot you are! Young Poland—my fledglings! One's got bandy legs and the other's got punctured lungs! Ha, ha!'

'I don't have bandy legs, Papa. I danced last week—I danced all week—'

'And look at you now. You'll never be a Galina. Never.'

He flicked the bend out of his paper. Anna glared at me. She was used to this. She turned to me then and said it was trivial of me to complain about a cough when Stalin had just died.

That evening, after Papa had gone to sleep, we drank cocktails of penicillin and vodka, and we made love on the kitchen floor. I went home and dreamt of the Sugarplum fairy dancing on a giant poster of Jozef Stalin. It was years before he really died.

Anna and I began to drink together. We drank and smoked until her ligaments and wings seized up completely. Finally she told Papa she could not go back to Warsaw. He would not speak to her. He put the picture of Stalin in a drawer, and hung Galina over the mantelpiece. We spent more time in St Bronislav's Street together. We stole afternoons and spent them wrapped around each other on this very chair I sit in, watching swans dip their necks into the river. Watching the Vistula snake its way past Wawel Castle, as I coiled her hair around my finger. Nestling my head in her chest, hearing the life beat through her swan's heart, under a veil of cream skin. Her cool hand clasping mine and sometimes clasping tightly. *Anna. Moja Kochana Anno.* Laughing as we made love, saying she was dancing. And the rush for clothes, in case she'd be late for Papa's tea.

Once I brought her home in the rain of a storm and we raced through the streets together, jumping over puddles, kissing under the wet trees. The thunder rumbling in the distance, like someone moving furniture around up in the sky, she said. Back in Chopin Street, Papa was nowhere to be found, but the kettle whined and the wireless whistled out, voices lost at sea. Where is Papa? Anna said, and secretly I hoped that he was dead. There, I said, under the table. Like a poor old dog, shivering under the table. Papa, scared to death of storms. He was hearing bombs drop out of the sky and tanks growling at him in the garden. He had his hands clasped over his ears and his eyes were shut. Praying, like Aunt Magdalena. After all that, he was afraid of storms. I felt fond of him again: Papa with his blazing little samovar and his wickedly strong cigarettes. Papa, waving at you through his smoky fog, laughing his horsy laugh at you until his eyes watered and he wheezed.

But he grew ill. His bones began to rot. There was cancer in his bone marrow. He rocked himself to sleep by his samovar, smoked a yellow stain onto the side of his mouth and wept over the things he'd never see: his mother, his wife, his socialist utopia. We stayed with him while death came closer. The great change was coming. His dying would be like a huge wall falling down.

Just before Papa's death, riots broke out in Nowa Huta. The authorities refused to allow a new church to be built. The People proclaimed that the Steelworks was not their God. Papa said, in a rasping whisper: *I would have built a church for them, I would have. To hell with the authorities, to hell with them.* He died holding a cross to his chest, with his daughter weeping dutifully by his bed, and the little samovar spluttering in the corner, where I had been keeping vigil in his last days.

14

There was a terrible silence after Papa Goralski left us. He had donated Chopin Street to the Party—I'm sure that if Anna had been a better Galina, he wouldn't have done that. But he did. Anna found herself an administrative job in the Academy of Music and moved in with me.

She was allowed a quota of work, which she was under strict orders never to exceed: to open two letters a day, to answer the phone once every hour. Any more than that and she was stealing work from another employee. Poor Anna. From dancing to immobility. I had begun to lecture in the School of Architecture, but the curricula were bound by state decree. These were the Disenchanted Years. We were bored when we woke up, bored when we went to sleep. There were no goals, no dreams, no deadlines. We lugged our load to the top of the hill and let it roll down the same side. Over, and over, and over again.

One month after her father died, at the end of a Golden October, I asked her to marry me.

'You want children, Stasiu?'

She thought I would steal her body, but I just wanted to give my memories to someone.

'Maybe one day.'

'You want to marry me?'

'Yes.'

'You want me to marry you?'

We were walking by the river with the castle behind us and dead leaves swimming around us, dry coloured paper crunching under our soles. It was near where we had met on my twelfth birthday, when she skated over to me in a blue scarf on the river.

'We will marry, Stanislav. You are all I have. I love you and you love me. That's all we have.'

I pressed her hand to mine and took it up to kiss it. I looked into her eyes: Wawel Castle and the trees in them. But there was a shadow there. I hoped it was not too late.

There was a small ceremony held in a registry office on a Wednesday. Jan was my witness. There were no flowers, no white veils; there was no music. It was our little victory over the Church. And the State's little victory over us. Joyless, silent victories. Papa's paltry legacy paid for our honeymoon. (Most of his money had been left to the ZSMP.) We went to the mountains and stayed in one of those odious government hostels with vomit-coloured walls.

It was a strange time of the year to get married. The beginning of November, when winter sets in. It was a time when we could only get vinegar with our food coupons. So we ate mountain cheese, and drank. We drank honeyed wine in a state-owned restaurant. It was one of those old Zakopane wooden houses with intricately carved furniture and bright coloured walls. One night she said to me: 'Stasiu, why don't we build a little house here in the mountains? We should get out of Aunt Magda's house. It depresses me. Why don't we get out?'

I had lost all interest in building, until that moment. When I had seen the monstrosities that beset our city, I lost all interest. Nowa Huta represented all that had been stolen from us in our sleep: the beauty of individuality. Stolen and made into grey blocks with grey streets and grey parks and yellow-grey smoke.

'We might, Anna, we might.'

'What do you mean, we might? We must!'

'Anna, these are hard times. There are a lot of traps. We need permission, we need help. If Papa was alive—'

'Oh, shut up. Obviously you're not alive. Dead old architect. You can't even build—you're just like Papa, God forgive me. I can't take it.'

'Take what, Ania?'

'You! You're dead! No! Not just you. Everything. Everyone. We're being killed with boredom. They've taken away from us what keeps us alive. I don't care that we are forbidden to consume but I cannot feel my soul. My dance is gone. I'm locked up in a yellow box in the Academy with an ugly brown lampshade hanging over my head all day and the endless tap of a typewriter and the phone rings once in a blue moon and the only colour there is a plastic fern in the far corner of the room pretending to grow. Everything is brown and grey, Stanislav. Let's get out of it. Let's get out. Let's go to your mother and brother in the West. Why not? What the hell have we got to lose?'

'It would be worse there, Ania.'

'Worse! What could be worse than this? If I stay here any longer I'll start going to church. Or I'll kill myself! I will!'

'You can go. I will not go.'

'You won't forget about the war. You want to stay in this sick purgatory. What about your family?'

'Too much time has passed. It wouldn't be the same.'

'You don't ever want to see them?'

'I didn't say that.'

'But do you?'

'I may—'

'Do you?'

'No. Never. I never want to see them again.'

Anna cried, so I promised her I'd build a house that I knew I'd never build. We stumbled out of the restaurant, onto the street. The stars were there in the sky. Like someone had shot holes in the dark. The moon was there. Had this always been there? I so rarely noticed. The brave sky showed me how tiny was my life and the sadness in it. Yes, Anna, I lied, I will build us a house.

It had begun to snow. My nose dripped, my head was singed by the cold. I clenched my numb fists in my coat pockets. We could see nothing ahead of us through the frantic snowflakes. We continued walking straight to the town, back to the government hostel. Anna and I curled up on the bed; her tears had dried up. She threw her arms around my waist and kissed my cheek. She was sorry that she had shouted. It was the wine, not her.

In the morning we climbed up the Widow's Mountain, and watched the river thunder down. On the way back Anna fell and gashed her knee on a rock. I swabbed the cut with my shirt. Anna, my fatherless wife. Who would she dance for now, with her hurt knee and all her fathers dead? We drank hot chocolate in silence and left the mountains.

We took an orange bus with chains on its wheels. Slow, clanking, faithful as reality always is. A man smoked stinking cigarettes in the seat behind us, coughing fitfully between each cigarette. We passed the streets of squat wooden Zakopane houses, their secrets covered in thick white snow. The orange bus brought us to the end of our honeymoon and the beginning of our wedded days. Faithful, as reality always is.

15

Anna wrapped her body in the silks and furs her mother had left behind. She was still beautiful. More beautiful, I thought, gliding through the Planty on a summer's day, with the hum of the bee and songs of the birds and the trees leaning over, whispering. Much more beautiful than she was on a wooden stage in a gaudy theatre, bound by the choreographer's symmetrical web. How her feet had bled.

We hung about in illegal jazz cafés where she boasted to my friends, through her brash cigarette smoke, that she was a dancer on sabbatical, much in demand. This, the artists said, was where freedom lived: in the cellars of Kraków. There you could exhibit your soul in an anarchic dream beneath ground level. The bastards couldn't get you down there.

Anna went underground. I stayed above. I detested the system as much as she but I had no interest in consorting with a bunch of drunken hooligans in the sewage pipes of our city.

Janusz Konwicki, a stout little artist from the Academy of Fine Arts, was the first to lick his chops around Anna. She was doing part-time life modelling in the Academy at the time. How her beauty made his pencil move! How gracefully she decked herself with her sheet at the end of a class! Once, after a class he fired his pencil to the floor. Its point pierced lightly into her right heel. She flicked her torso down and, with her head almost between her knees, took the pencil from the floor with a long, elegant sweep of her arm. She had her sheet around her, of course. No doubt it fell off, or it nearly fell off, in some erotic fashion, to Konwicki's delight. Whatever happened, he was very pleased.

That evening, he kissed her hand and led her down the twisting stone steps of a stone cellar in Kazimierz. He kissed her hand and begged to see her dance. She did, plied with vodka, stretching the seams of her thick nylon trousers. They had found their dancer. She coughed her guts raw in the black candle smoke and laughed as vodka gushed through her veins. They loved her. She would be the muse of their artistic revolution.

One night, I went to see Anna perform in a cellar on Szczpanska Street. How Poland loves keeping secrets. Secrets locked in dens, crypts, cellars and caves. Secret, conspiratorial meetings in the night are the habit of a bullied nation. The trouble is, I hate our country's secrets. I hate its pickled food, its Virgin Marys, its communism, its anti-communism, its love of pork, its love of Jews, its hatred of Jews, its dumplings and its pigs' trotters.

As I was descending the hundred stone steps, I felt a thrill of excitement in my empty stomach, as the smoke got thicker and muffled voices louder. Artists milled about in garish costumes. Konwicki smirked when I appeared in the archway: me, in my brown flannels, among the city's peacocks. Stanislav the architect, who couldn't build.

I found Anna in the changing room with a bear at her back, tugging up her zip. She had hairpins in her mouth and lipstick on her hands and no time for me. It all smacked of the day I tried to take her hand outside the Warsaw Ballet Theatre. Piotr Salicki, the great Master of Ceremonies, appeared before me, smoking a long cigarette and holding, in the same hand as his cane, a small bottle of foreign vodka. He wore a handlebar moustache. Under

[65]

his wide-brimmed black hat, a grey rat's tail dangled down his back. He was a tall, broad man and he wore a cape that made him taller. I had seen him, slinking about the town like a swarthy pimpernel. He was, they said, the greatest male muse that our rich and ancient city had beheld. The authorities turned a blind eye.

'Pan Malinski, welcome to our cave, welcome.' He took off his black hat, and swept it beneath him, holding my gaze with his sad, merry eyes. The feather in his hat brushed against my hand as he swept the hat back up to his head.

'Won't you have a drink, Pan Malinski?' He brought me through another arch, around a corner, to a darkened corner of the cabaret, with a gargoyle leaning over us and a Prussian army helmet staring at us. I accepted the vodka. Salicki toasted me and winked, as if to say, *it's all right now, you're one of us.* I'd heard about Salicki and his fondness for young men and I was not about to get drawn into his web. But he drew me in, regardless, on his invisible silver rope. He was impossible to resist. In an insane moment, with the third large gulp of vodka burning in my throat, I thought: *I love this man, I'll give him anything he needs.*

'Anna,' he said, 'your wife.' As if to remind me. 'She is our best dancer. We could not have done this without her.' Another voice, coming from somewhere under his beard, said *Please don't take her away from us.* Then, as if at his command, Anna walked in, looking like a worn-out marionette. She leaned against the archway, and clasped her hand around her Master's shoulder.

'Hello, Stanislav,' she said, and planted her hand on her hip, flirting. 'I'm so glad you came. You know he doesn't approve of us, Piotr! He's only come to check us out. Like the Secret Police. Haven't you, Stasiu?' I froze into my brown flannels, and said absolutely nothing. Someone was playing the saxophone under another gargoyle, somewhere. I lunged into my vodka.

'Anna,' said Piotr, 'me and Pan Malinski, we were just talking—isn't it time you—?'

She left and I heard her swan's heart pit-a-pat, hurt by the little scold she'd got. Salicki smiled, and offered me a Gauloise.

Ten o'clock. A bony, unshaven creature sitting at a piano
begins racing his fingers up and down a melancholy E-flat scale.
Janusz Konwicki sits beaming in the front row with his arms
folded over his fat belly. A painting of a dancer is spotlighted.
There is silence, then darkness, then light. A giant Soviet flag is
draped over the painting. There is movement under the flag;
something fighting to break free. The dancer's head emerges out
of the flag, like a baby's head pushing between its mother's bloody
legs. Anna. Her body struggles under the thick canvas flag. She
moves to the side. The painting is revealed. The dancer has been
cut out, leaving only her contour. Anna struggles on. An arm
breaks out (no doubt the arm with which Konwicki fell in love).
Another arm breaks out (the one he didn't love so much). All the
time the piano thunders up and down the scale, like wind gash-
ing against a huge mountain. Anna's torso breaks free into
incredible convulsions as she waves her arms back and forth in
rapid sweeping motions. Finally, the flag is flung to the audience.
Anna, dressed in a white ballet costume, crowned by a feather
headpiece, breaks into voluptuous movement. The hysterical
pianist stops in mid-note. Silence resumes. Anna is squashed into
the contour of the canvas dancer. Light fades. Darkness resumes.
A great impression has been made.

When they clapped, they clapped for Salicki, not for Anna. It
was to him they were devoted, not her. Salicki had taken all his
little protégés in under his generous wing, promising to bring

them back to life again. You see, that's what they said he did: he brought dead things to life again. It was he who, after Stalin's death, had lit the way down to this unused dusty cellar, hunched beneath the Square. From here he rounded up the city's quivering artistic souls, gave them licence to satirize the idiots upstairs. And they adored him for it. Even the Secret Police were seen to glow when he rang his little bell between the acts.

16

How shall Henryk and I greet each other? When he comes in through my door, will I fling my full-grown arms around him? I have had this image of our awkward meeting at the door, there, speechless after forty-nine years of utter silence. I forgot: he does not know this city, I shall have to meet him at the station. I have no idea what he looks like.

What shall I feed him? I cannot feed him those pre-historic preserves. I tried some, the other day. The cucumbers nauseated me, as pre-war cucumbers should. The rubber seals on the jars have cracked and turned brown. What a fool I am. I had an image of us sitting together at the table, plunging our hands into the cloudy jars, pulling out the cucumbers. I must be practical. I cannot take him out to the milk bars to eat; he will think I'm lazy. I will have to cook. What will he eat? What has he been eating for forty-nine years? Did he marry? Will he judge me for not having a family? He will understand me, surely.

Jan has saved me once again. Today I went shopping and I bought some vegetables, beans and pork. I had no idea how they could be assembled into something edible. What gruel could I make from them? Then Jan came along. He caught me fondling a turnip on a stall near the Market Square. It was a dirty turnip, caked with earth. The peasant woman on the stall had a similar complexion—purple and soiled. She quoted a low price and cackled through her brazen, toothless grin, reminding me of peasants at Pinsk Market, where Mama once brought Henryk and me. The peasant woman said I couldn't get a better turnip in the city. Look at the size of it, she said. Never mind the dirt, that's only earth. Good earth. Go on … one thousand zlotys. I wondered would my brother eat this thing that had been nurtured by contaminated Polish earth, hurled into a filthy shit-stained van and deposited into this woman's wooden box. What could I do with a turnip? What could Henryk do with a turnip? What, collectively, could we do with a turnip?

'A beauty, Stanislav. Buy it,' said Jan.

'You think so?'

'Yes! A fine size.'

'But what will I do with it? How will I make it into food?'

'You mustn't panic, Stanislav. You still have time to learn to cook.'

'That's all very well, Jan. It's all very well to joke. But I have three days. Three days! I have not seen him in forty-nine years and he will be here in three days. And tomorrow it will be two. And the next day one. And you tell me not to panic?'

'Stanislav, buy this turnip and we will teach you to cook.'

We took the tram to Prondnik Bialy, where Jan lives with his family. He lives on the seventh floor of a tower block. They're building a new church nearby. We sat together on his balcony. We sat smoking and drinking lemon tea. A flock of ravens sailed over us, cawing. They swooped beneath the trees. I said I had always seen these things as omens. Jan stroked his moustache and chuckled.

'My friend, for an enemy of the Church you are too superstitious. The ravens are only trying to sing.'

There is something comforting in Jan's paternalism. He looks a bit rabbinical, when he talks like that. Perhaps he is a Jew: perhaps he managed to fool even me. I told him about Henryk's letter. The ravens flew around the tower block again. Then they flew off and we watched them get as small as a crowd of black bees.

'Your brother. Jesus Mary. Coming here? What will he think of this place?'

'He will think it a miserable pit. And that we are miseries in it. He will be glad he got out—'

'But you forget. We are independent now. This is a liberated country. You should be proud!'

'And what change is there? You know. Revolution eats its own children. We are still queuing but we have no one to blame any more. Now we can see western produce. They put it here to taunt us. Who the hell can afford it?'

'Revolution has eaten *you*, Stanislav. You are not blind or stupid. This is a time of transition. Are you afraid of freedom?'

'It is not freedom! We still have the Church breathing down our backs.'

'So you prefer it the way it was? Waiting for Godot? Now you have Godot and you're still miserable.'

'I don't want to show my brother this miserable place.'

'What about Wawel Castle, the Tatra Mountains, the Gothic churches?'

'I'm not going to traipse around the place with him. I have no time. I have no energy. My lungs will act up.'

A petal fell from the potted geranium, and slid down off the toe of my shoe.

'You don't deserve to meet him.'

'You don't understand. It is *his* fault that we were separated. He willed it.'

I told Jan the story of the red toy train. He laughed again and rubbed his moustache. He said nothing in response to my story. It was as if he knew something about destiny that I did not.

Then he did what he rarely does. He brought me to his kitchen. This was where I had first met his wife twenty years ago, the inner sanctum of the family. This was where she had judged me an unshaven, agnostic widower, as she handed me a glass of cold coffee and smiled unwillingly. It was the day after Anna had left us.

Those days came back to me again: how life was then, with Anna. How I used to take myself to the Technical University every day, clutching my papers, terrified of losing Anna. Every day, terrified of losing Anna. I in an eyrie, she in a cave. She hated my brown and sometimes blue suits, my imitation leather shoes, my wheezing lungs. How I came home to her boiled dinners and talked about buttresses and rib-vaults: I lived in the thirteenth century and she did not. It eased my pain, you see, to leap about in the vaults of Gothic churches, tucked away safely centuries before the war and this whole mess. I hung like a bat from Gothic arches when I was supposed to be queuing for meat.

One muggy July night Anna did not come home. I drowned my coffee in vodka and scratched myself to sleep as a warm nauseating breeze blew the curtains in (as if some cretin was sitting on the balcony with an electric fan). There was a stone in my belly. This betrayal would divide us for good. There would not be children now, and I would never build.

She came home at seven o'clock in the morning, just as I was leaving to go to work. Her head hung, uncharacteristically, over her chest. The rest was a ghastly cliché.

'Who is it?'

'There's no one.'

And so on.

She had left her Stanislav without his evening meal, and left him in the bed alone. Piotr Salicki had invited her to a ball. People streamed in from all parts of the city, from outside the city to that tiny little cellar under the Market Square. For such a small, hidden place, the cabaret had a devastating reputation. And Anna was their dancer. But Salicki had limited her repertoire to something pitiful. Each night, she was hoisted to the ceiling in her tutu, suspended by a rope attached to a thick leather belt around her waist. If only her father could have seen her, swinging from the rafters like a cheap Christmas fairy with her cheeks painted red, mascara-clotted lashes, her face thick with theatrical muck.

'You never did understand,' she said, 'that I have to dance.'

'That is not dancing, Anna.'

'You never understood. And you never will.'

'May your father haunt you,' I said.

'May we divorce?' she said.

'Certainly,' I said.

But we had tea, instead. Anna wept into my blue sleeve, and made it damp. *Could we please, please go west? I don't want to be a flying doll, Stasiu! I want to be famous and have money and a real house and I want an English breakfast!* They found, when she was lowered to the ground after an evening's swing, that she could not walk. She was blind drunk. She was always blind drunk, in that den. And no, I never did find out if she had spent the night in the arms of some Konwicki or not. It only mattered that she had come back to me.

'Stanislav, you're dreaming,' said Jan.

'Not dreaming. Remembering. Do you remember that man from the cellar on the square? The one with the black moustache?'

'I still go to that cabaret sometimes. He's still there. You should bring Henryk, eh?'

'I might.'

Jan took me back to the kitchen and sat me down. His wife had laughed at the notion of my cooking a meal. I still had that lost, academic look about me and that meant poison in the kitchen. She offered, perhaps to put an end to our silent war, to cook for Henryk and me for the time that he was here. I thanked her. She blessed me. It was a redeeming moment for us both. She had at last forgotten Anna. And so, perhaps, would I.

I wonder what Henryk will think of this dilapidated abode of mine? It's like a shipwreck. The authorities have been saying it is structurally unsound for over fifty years. Just as my aunt ignored them, I have ignored them. Nobody has ever ordered us to evacuate. The wooden beams are riddled with dry rot. Some of the slats on the stair have cracked under my very feet. The same stairs that the rosy German officer and his band of merry men climbed on the Eve of All Saints, 1942. There is a window that stretches up from the ground floor to the second. Its frame is of thick rusting steel. The walls here are a blistered turquoise blue. The ceilings are yellow, stained with clouds of black mould, much like the insides of Papa Goralski's lungs. This is my building and I shall never move from it. The beams may cave in, the stairs may collapse into the cellar, but I will never leave. It was here that I survived. Henryk may say what he likes about the ugly walls and the suspicious tower. This is my home and this is where he shall stay while he is in Poland.

But why, oh Henryk, are you coming to me just as my home is about to capsize into the river? And with Anna gone away?

17

We never did divorce. The disease pre-empted us: Anna was diagnosed with cancer of the liver. Something menacing and greedy, but not male, had taken control of her body. She anaesthetized herself with secret donations of vodka that would appear from under her visitors' coats. That included my own. Sometimes we drank together in merry, glazed denial. We thought we were delaying the inevitable. But sober hours made the smell of disinfectant and dying bodies so much more harsh. Sometimes I could not talk at all. I would sit there listening to the clock tick in the corridor, watching the paint peel off the cast-iron bed, knowing it would all have to outlive her.

I held her limp, cold hand every day until she died. I could see the malignant parasite consuming her from inside, sucking life out of her with steady, gruelling intent. Visitors came, handing her pity with their flowers. They were no comfort to her. She hated the pretence that they could console her out of death. When they left, their flowers turned brown at the edges and lost their aroma to the big bully smell of disinfectant.

She was ashamed to have her shrinking yellow body visited by Piotr Salicki. He who had hoisted her drunken body into the vaults of that cellar. And had seen her fall, wizened and angered, to this wretched state. Never mind, they came and went, these temperamental artists. The wings were bursting with the misfits of the State.

She died in the middle of the night one Monday, outside visiting hours. When I saw her body it seemed the pain had left it. She had that docile look that she'd lost in recent years. Anna, my Marxist ballerina, my second greatest traitor. I loved her as I had loved my Mama.

The day the riots broke out and Anna's death—those two events hold hands. March 1968. She'd left me to contend with this. Her death and the riots. It was bleak. I hardly noticed the riots. There were truncheons and water guns and barricades around the city's old walls, but I never noticed. I stayed in my room with the vodka that Anna had left me. A few days later I was interrogated by a committee of pallid administrators who looked as if they'd slept their lives away in filing cabinets. They had got it into their heads that my lecture series, 'Ideological influences on architecture from the Gothic to the Modern', smacked of the counter-revolutionary. They ran their fingers through their greasy hair and insisted that I was mocking progressive socialism. I had outlined the significant influence that Marxist ideology had had on post-war architecture. I persuaded them that it was for the benefit of socialism that I had proposed my argument.

One of them turned a page on his clipboard and threw at me the inevitable non sequitur: did I have any Jewish relatives? They did not take my word. They ordered me to deliver to their office the next morning documents that verified my case. This I did, and I never heard another word from the authorities. I suppose they found better scapegoats for the country's social, economic and political chaos.

I was in decline. I became the sort of man who carries with him a yellowish, crumpled handkerchief. Whose collars have a dark grey rim. Whose glasses are encrusted with dandruff. Whose index finger is yellow, whose fingernail has small brown stripes running up the centre. In short, I had become a widower. Things I could not control began to descend on me, like this lymph node and this seizured finger and my loosening teeth. Anna was gone. I had always thought that I would go first.

I gave up eating. What was the point? A few years after Anna died the price of meat rose by seventeen per cent. The queues were endless. I was happier to lace my numbered days with booze. I sold my meat vouchers to that end. Those were days I don't want to remember. Sauntering unsteadily by the frozen Vistula, remembering little Anna in her blue scarf and her eyes that had no nightmares. I wept under a tree. I was found, there, by the police. They took me away and put me in a cell. I was ashamed. I am still ashamed. Jan gave them a bottle of vodka and brought me home.

Mama wrote to me some time in the early seventies. She was ever so sorry about my wife. But was it not wonderful, she said, that Poland was opening up? Poles were travelling abroad a lot these days. Would I ever come to Ireland? I did not respond. We were opening up, all right. An invasion of privately owned Fiat 126s had hit the streets. Fleets of them were pelting around with large Polish men squashed up against the windscreens, excreting low-octane petrol fumes, delightedly, into the acid fog. Things soon got worse again. Inflation rose and the little cars became an indispensable means of transport to the nearest queue for food.

I came home one day and found a peasant woman in a shawl dragging a bloody sack up my stairs.

'Meat, sir. Do you want some?'

'No, thank you.'

'You want to queue?'

'I never queue and I never eat. Please stop smearing my stairs with blood.'

She scowled and dragged her sack of meat back down the stairs. Thump, thump, thump. My neighbour would buy some. The whole of Kraków would buy some if they could get their hands on it. I had better things to do.

Slowly, but surely, things were falling apart. Cigarettes and matches disappeared. The factories could not afford spare parts for their machines. I shook for days with nicotine withdrawals and took to rummaging in public bins to satisfy my habit. I would follow smokers in the street, walking in the trail of that luxurious blue smoke, sniffing it up my starving nostrils.

Mama wrote again when John Paul took the throne. There, I have something to thank the Pope for. I had been attending to the changes in my body and the changes in my country. I had expelled my brother and my mother to the periphery of my consciousness. I blinked. I closed my eyes. I tried to remember what they looked like. But the images I sought had drowned. The contours bled into other, more recent faces. Anna. Anna and her Papa. They had been my family. It was they whom I missed.

18

One day left before he comes. Jan came to see me today. He put his foot through one of the steps. I became hysterical. Not because of the step, but because of what it implied: I am living in a near-derelict building. My brother is coming in one day and I have not seen him in forty-nine years and he may put his foot through one of my steps!

'Calm down.' Jan patted my back.

'What can I do? What can I do? My brother is coming tomorrow and my house is falling down and I am an old man. Tomorrow! He's coming tomorrow. I cannot see him when my house is like this.'

'You could telephone him and ask him to come a few days later. Does he have a telephone?'

'What does it matter if he does? I don't! I've been waiting twenty years in this pit for a telephone!'

'Stanislav, we'll go to the post office and phone him.'

We took the tram to the centre. I decided to buy some groceries and cigarettes before we went to the post office to phone. There was a strange man in the grocer's. He had pale blank eyes and a large nose. He wore a navy beret and he shuffled around the shop with his fist clamped around his precious plastic bag.

'Buongiorno, Signorita!' he cried. The cashier scowled at him and tapped her pen on the counter.

'Madame, I have come for the candles. *Gli Candelli*. So, now, may I see?'

'The only candles we have here are the ones we have for power cuts. Not for sale. This is a grocery store, not a church.'

'This is Florianska number thirty-two. You are the candle

specialist. I have travelled a long way today to see your candles. Why have you hidden them away?'

'You're in the wrong place, sir.'

'Florianska number thirty-two.'

'The wrong place.'

'Ah, madame.'

His eyes sank into his empty bag: a parched man gazing into an empty well.

'There is nothing in my bag. Do you have any nuts?'

'Over there.'

'Ah, yes. Thank you. Thank you so much. Thank you for your time. Thank you.'

At his point I intervened. I took him from the dazzling row of detergents to which he had wandered, over to the nuts which he claimed he was looking for.

'Thank you, sir. Is this—Florianska number thirty-two?'

'It is.'

'That's funny. I was here last week on a pilgrimage and I bought my candles here. I think there is something very strange going on. Things are changing very quickly, don't you think? Do you know that young lady?'

'Sir, if my memory serves me right, this was where my aunt used to buy candles for her private masses. It closed down some time during the war.'

'Ah, yes. That would be right. That's right. Oh dear. Now, where are the nuts? Have you seen them? You see I forgot my watch again. How much are they? How much are they? I cannot see. Let's see now, let's see.'

He took two packets from the shelf and dropped them into his bag. His eyes fell down after them, and a shadow moved over him. He paid for the nuts. The cashier threw the change at him from her side of the gulf. He thanked her profusely again and shuffled out, clutching his bag of nuts.

Outside, he stopped. He hunched his shoulders, tightened his grip on the bag and stared ahead.

'Why,' he asked, 'is so much gone?'

'We'll find you another candle, sir.'

'Ah, but this was a special scene … Snow was falling, *pit-a-pat-a-pit-a-pat.*'

He closed his eyes and danced his fingers up and down, imitating the snow in his mind. He forced the memory on, but the street was indifferent to his nostalgia: people nudged irritably past the nutcase waving his hands. The buildings stood disdainfully erect.

'*Pit-a-pat-a-pit-a-pat.* Like that. Beautiful. Near Christmas, 1940. And so, you see, I had to paint. And how? How could I do that?! My paints would smudge! For sure they would smudge! So I came here to this little candle shop and they gave me some wax. Here, Florianska number thirty-two. I took my wax and executed my work … I sketched it in the wax with the snow falling over my fingers and the Nazis marching all about. The Planty in the snow. *Pit-a-pat-a-pit-a-pat.* It was a very fine piece—it was, well, so big.' We left him throwing his nuts at the pigeons.

Jan and I took off in the direction of the Main Post Office. I clutched Henryk's letter in my pocket. I prayed that he would not die in the aeroplane and I prayed that he would. The cow behind the glass would not tell us the code to Ireland.

'There is none.'

'Of course there is!'

'I don't know. Ask at the other desk.'

She went back to polishing her nails. We huddled into the booth. There was no light so I lit a match. The nail polisher marched over and swung the door open to tell us it was forbidden to light matches in the booths.

'But we can't see!'

'You are creating a hazard.'

After she went I nearly set the letter on fire. We dialled the number seventeen times, connecting with the same unfortunate local number every time. But at last an unfamiliar ringing tone came to my ears.

'Hello? Is this Ireland?'

'There's no one of that name living here.'

'Excuse—me?'

A wave of crackling interference drowned the voice.

'Hallo? Is Henryk there?'

'Just a minute.'

The crackling sounded in again, like a low flying plane. I lost the voice completely. I knew it would not work. I couldn't really conceive of making contact with a country that far away. The nail-preener took twenty thousand zlotys from me and told me not to light matches in the booth the next time I made a phone call in a public booth.

'There won't be a next time.'

I walked home by the Planty and Wawel Castle and down by the river again. It is an exquisite time of year for Henryk to visit. This golden October will welcome him, if nothing else. The swans are looking clean and beautiful for him. Perhaps he won't smell the sulphur dioxide. His pores will soak it in and his lungs will breathe it in without his knowing. His eyes will water and his head will spin and he will feel a tightening in his chest. However, that is not my fault. I am not to blame. Perhaps it was he who answered the phone. Perhaps he could not understand me. Perhaps we no longer speak the same language. War does that and did worse. Some lost their bodies but I still have mine, trampled as it is, home to these deformities. Henryk still has his. All these years, punctuated by tomorrow. He's damn lucky the Soviets have gone. Poland is free. And so am I, I suppose.

2

Henry

I

I like to blast the windows open and roar out a greeting to the world when the snowdrops have opened their little beaks and the leaves have burst out of their pods. I like to be in the city in the springtime, sauntering around the place, watching people peddling their wares, listening to people tear each other to pieces in the pubs. I have learned to accept that after we rise, we fall. I've spent my whole life leaping about and crashing down again. What I've learned is that when you crash you have to do it in the right spot. In a woman's lap, for instance. I've learned to get the timing right.

People don't think much of me, really. They seem to object. They only remember the Henry that insulted them, that made a presumptuous pass at them, that crooned his medley when they wanted to have a quiet chat. I know I am obnoxious. But that's the only way they'll know I'm there.

They know I'm going to Poland, but they don't know I'm going *back*. Nobody knows that. They all think I was born and bred here, those friends of mine. They've never even heard of the place I'm from: Lvov. They're better off not knowing; it would just confuse their little heads. As the Fool says:

> *Speak less than thou knowest,*
> *Have less than thou owest,*
> *Keep thy whore in-a-door*

That is my creed. This is my old sod, too. To hell with geneal-ogy—it's where you've breathed and farted all your life that mat-ters. I'm sounding morbid and it's only ten in the morning. Ten in the morning of the morning that I am to buy my ticket back to Poland. I'm getting a cheap deal with a crowd on Capel Street called Zip Travel, run by a Hungarian count, of all the things. He imports paprika on the side. I have to fly through Dresden, of all the godforsaken places. Back to Poland, to see old Stanislav again. Poor old Stan, stuck out there all that time. And he hardly wrote! That upset Mummy, it really did.

2

Not only do I have no idea what Stanislav looks like, I have no idea what he *looked* like either. All I remember is that there was-n't much of him. Everything back there is dominated by the shadow of Hilbig. I can't see little old Stan at all. We should have exchanged photographs, but that would have declared our estrangement with an almighty roar. What a corny idea, exchanging photographs, like teenage pen-pals. We are middle-aged veterans of war, God bless us!

I remember my mother sniffling over a box of photographs on the train that took us out of Poland. God knows what happened to them. Funny old Mummy. We were a bit estranged ourselves, after all that happened. You'd think we'd have been united by our experiences. Neither of us ever confessed anything to each other. Hilbig the Humbug. I hope the Nuremberg Trials had him sent to hell.

I know I loved my father. I know I hunted butterflies for him, and laid them on his desk like the morning shrew a loyal cat brings its master. He used to sweep them off the desk, thinking they had died there in the night. He didn't know his little Henry loved him so. When the war came, he said he loved Poland and left us forever. That meant that he did not love us, and that he never came back was living proof of it. He was a hunter and a man of letters. That might seem strange, but that was him. A well-bred savage. I remember coming across a little samovar on Francis Street a few years ago, and how it put the heart crossways in me. It was as if I had found a lost part of my anatomy. I pictured my father, his hands covered in grease for the gun, blood on his cuffs. And I remembered a vile piece of sinew I found once on the floor, the gooey remnant of his booty before the taxidermist got to work. There I was in an antique market on Francis Street, gazing like an idiot at this samovar. The owner, forgivably, assumed I wished to buy the thing. He couldn't even tell me what it was.

'It's one of those contraptions for heating water, from Turkey or Greece or somewhere. I'll give it to you for a fiver.'

You can stick your contraption up your arse, mister. I marched out, left my father in the spout. I thought that was the end of it but as I turned onto Kevin Street, pastries and tea and mead and pickles appeared before my inner eyes. And some maid with a big arse. Horses. Dead deer. Howling dogs. Bastard cold. Skating on a snowing day. The past conspired against me. But I put things right. I went on a binge that made me forget my own name. When I awoke, my new set of problems promptly pushed the old ones out of the way.

If anybody knew the truth about me they'd have me locked in the zoo. My mother made me to go to confession but I didn't like those black and white priests. I went, all right. I took myself obediently to the box and I begged for blessings and atonements for my invented sins: stealing a bag of sweets, thinking bad thoughts about my stepfather. But not for what I'd really done. They'd have flung me right into the fires of hell for that. I complied, but I lied. I did it for my mother.

Poor old Stan got left behind. But he didn't have too bad a time of it, up in Cracow eating Aunty Magda's cakes while we were locked up at home with the enemy prodding the poker into us from our own fire. We quartered, me and my mother, with the enemy. We made tea for the occupiers in the pause between slaughter and massacre. Mumsy's fault. She dragged me back to the house to grab her hats before the next batch of looters moved in. But we were too late. Hilbig had pre-empted us. We walked straight into his lair. My mother was determined that the Nazis would not wear her hats around the house. The martyrs to the summer hat collection strolled down the drive, waving to the tanks as they did, tra-la-la, to the house that was smothered in red and black banners in honour of their visit. *We'd-just-like-to-pick-up-a-few-things-we-left-behind-we-hope-you-don't-mind-it's-just-that-we-didn't-know-you'd-be-moving-in-so-soon-and-how-are-you-settling-in?*

[88]

My mother was an insanely polite woman. Hans Hilbig, SS Oberscharführer of Lvov, was rather taken aback. How had these biologically inferior Poles managed to sneak past the laser eyes of the Reich?

I was beaten and thrown into the dining room with the chickens and my mother was dragged by her straw-coloured hair to the hall, had her head gashed against the wall under my father's boars' heads. They raped her in front of me. After the chickens had been evacuated, they threw her into the dining room with me. Over the next few days the bones of the chickens were thrown to us through a crack in the door.

Hilbig boomed in the day my mother was about to eat her rosary beads. He threw bread on the floor and we devoured it like famished dogs. A tiny piece of stucco fell from the ceiling when Hilbig slammed the door. I ate that too. I thought it was a piece of icing from some giant cake we couldn't see.

'Guten Morgen, Fräulein!'

The sun was blazing outside, and Hilbig was in top form, delighted with his morning prey. He had enjoyed the evening with my mother. It would suit him to have her around, especially since she knew the language of the Reich. But the boy, he would have to be silent until he learnt his German. Polish was forbidden.

I suppose we were lucky. His first impulse had been to shoot us. His second had been to send us off to Belzec Labour Camp. But unlike most of the Polish dog-race, we could be of use about the house. Besides, my mother had those cornflower eyes … when he told her that he ran his dry sausage finger under her chin and chuckled to himself until a cough attacked him.

Hilbig went to a lot of trouble for us. In an afternoon of

paperwork, his bureaucrats had turned out a thirty-seven-page Ahnentafel, a genealogical table that went back six generations to 1750, falsely proving us to be of German descent. We, the fictional Volksdeutsche, acquired patrician ancestors of high Hamburg society. My fabricated great great grandfather had lived in frugal solidity under the beams of a vast and sombre mansion on the east bank of the Elbe. He had married a Polish countess and she had brought him to Lvov. Hilbig was having a field day! He'd really fallen for my mother. With the Volksdeutsche papers complete, he marched up to her and patted her on the head.

'Now we can produce beautiful German babies.'

We belonged to Hilbig. We served his men. Men that ate and belched and roared in our dining room, that took pretty peasants to our bedrooms, that poached our fowl. Men that bathed in our baths and shat in our loos. We rose at five every morning. We cooked, we cleaned, we scrubbed, we dug, we planted, we raked, Mama baked, I chopped the wood and broke twigs over my red, scabby knees. We nibbled at lettuce leaves and raw potatoes in the garden, hoping to God Hilbig's men would not catch us. On Sundays we were given meat if there was any to spare. Hilbig had carried with him from his Lutheran church a curious reverence for the Day of Rest. Sometimes on a Sunday, in the lull between battles, we were locked into the schoolroom to have instruction in the discipline of Racial Science. This, said Hilbig, was the only way for us become truly German. He had plans to bring us back to Germany after the war, to have us 're-incorporated' into the Fatherland. Dear old Hilbig, looking after our best interests.

In class, our instructor (usually a worn-out cadet) compared Slavonic and German birth rates. He analyzed the average qualities of the Eastern European races (just what was it that made us so dog-like?) and had us discuss the threat to Nordic races posed by the biological inferiority of the Slavs. Had we heard of Alfred Rosenberg? No? Well, this great man proposed some great theories on the matter. So much so that the Führer appointed him Minister for the Occupied Eastern Territories. If I ever spoke Polish in the presence of my instructor, I got the whip. There are marks on my bottom to this day. I have no choice but to associate my mother tongue with pain, and so I am no longer fluent in that tongue.

We were given ample opportunity to put the theory of racial science into practice. Every day Hilbig, Official Confessor, would drag suspected Jews into his office. He wore that same weary, delirious look that my father had after a good day's hunting. I remember a woman shaking like one of Papa's rabbits outside Hilbig's office.

'Please,' she blubbered, 'help me.' But I could not. Her bruised eyes begged me. Her hooked nose, that would lead her to her death. Her false papers damp and crumpled in her epileptic fist. Hilbig opened the door to his office and sighed.

'Next!' he said, with wave of his arm. He looked like an overworked G.P. at the end of a hard day in the surgery. It was three in the afternoon. This Jewess was number sixty-seven. He closed the door. I heard her pleading, then *slap. Slap. Slap. Slap.* He threw her out the door to a buck-toothed officer who took her to the orchard. Then *bang.* She was gone. Just like that. He had to, you see. He was under orders: *clean up the eastern territories, raise the banners.* Number sixty-eight went in with his hands behind his back. A peasant, not a Jew. He was sent to Belzec with a blue star for stealing a piece of meat.

Let me ask a question. Was Hilbig just a savage Jew-hunting

Führer-worshipper? Because, I confess, I liked him. He abused us, he whipped us, he threatened to shoot us, he stole everything we owned. But old softy Henry still liked him. Why? Because he made me feel special. He chose me for the Super Race. To a little boy of seven whose dead father had been devoted solely to his samovar and his game, the Oberscharführer was attentive in comparison. There were times, when he had me on his knee, singing the songs of the Fatherland, when I felt it thrilling to be German. It was only when he drank the local vodka that he set his darker beast on us.

3

Tra-la-la, and there is a hup-la in there somewhere too. I am looking forward to getting out of this parochial bees' nest. Prying and wheedling are the great arts of this city, arts that put wings on the heels of our literary giants. Stifling. But I'm a bit of a gossip myself.

When I have had more than a couple of brandies (which I'm very fond of indeed), the ranter in me comes out. They say I'm a moaner, they say I'm a ranter. They hate it when I sing my songs. Old Henry doesn't feel as Irish as he'd like to feel. Something holds him back. Sometimes I feel a bit of a stranger. Sometimes. When the brandy brings on the melancholy. When the mornings are grim. When I am in a bare, open field, alone. I would like to invite a collection of my most intimate friends for dinner one evening, to feed them delicately sweetened meats, mange-touts, golden sauteed potatoes. I would like to pour vintage wine down their gullets, sweeten them up with coffee and petit-fours, and tell them, one by one, what happened. They wouldn't believe what happened. They'd think it was one of my stories. Most of these people never saw a Nazi in their life. Nazis here are as mythical as snakes and wolves and bears. I don't want anyone to know how I acquired impeccable German before I ever walked through Trinity's gates. They'd just think it was old Henry telling his tall stories again.

Mummy and I were not allowed to leave the house except to scrape the earth in search of vegetables that would not obey the pace of war. They emerged, indolently, out of the earth. Inside, the Führer hung below my father's boars' heads in the long hall. Hilbig insisted that I hail the Führer each time I passed him by. The wild pigs looked far fiercer to me. They had always looked fierce. They were the demons of the forest that roved in packs along the forest's spine. I believed, when a tank went roaring past the house, that a pack of sharp-fanged wolves were growling inside, ravenous, drooling for a piece of freshly dripping flesh. I was not far wrong.

The world had grown very dark by November 1941. Winter froze the German tank engines, paralyzed their weapons, shook their troops blue in the trenches. My mother coughed her guts raw. Her eyes went red and bulged. One night, when the house was wrapped in quiet snow, Hilbig, swollen with vodka, found my fevered mother in the hall. She was leaning against the Führer, wheezing like a bellows. Hilbig came up to her and cupped his broad leathery hands around her shoulders. He looked, with his green diluted eyes, into hers.

'Elizabet, my darling, you cannot slouch like that beside the Führer.'

With an agile, gentle movement, he scooped her into his

arms. He leaned his head down and rubbed his cheek against her forehead. Her eyes had closed. I had never seen him do that to her before. It seemed, then, that he had always wanted to do it. He brought her to the drawing room and put her on his knee, on the large black leather armchair that did not belong to the house. He poured teacups of vodka down her throat while he stroked her dampened forehead.

'For medicine, my little cat.'

She awoke and her cough came thundering back. He looked at her in horror and flung her to the floor, and set about his duties. He kicked her in the chest, left her groaning and spluttering on the floor. He swigged at his bottle, crooning Schubert ditties down the corridor, and as he passed the Führer he lowered his head, atoning for his love of a Slavic being. Wearily, he climbed the stairs and when he was halfway up, he swung himself around the newel post, lost his footing, and slithered down the stairs, ingeniously holding the bottle upright as he did. *Aaaaaaaaaah*, he said on his way down, bumping on the steps. *Aaaaaaaaaah*, very quietly, with his mouth wide open. He landed at the bottom, with his legs spread out over the bearskin, and there he fell asleep. His staff assistant dragged him up the stairs to bed, like an overtired child. Mama said later, I wonder what his wife would think.

What would my friends say? Like Oliver. Ollie's been a good steady friend over the years. He's been there enough times to get me out of the soup. Ollie, after he has butchered verbally the Christian Brothers, has cast the Pope into the pyre of his hatred, is usually ready for a good evening. Oliver is my closest friend. But as it is with everybody else, I sneak away at a certain point. Once, I was not able to accompany Oliver to his place of pain. It all spilled out one night by the Royal Canal.

We were gutted drunk after closing one night. We dribbled a few songs out by the canal. For old time's sake. It was too much for our sodden bodies. We took our brown paper bags to a bench and sat down. The swans made us look even more like bowsies. And then Oliver said with awful clarity that he was going to tell me something he'd never told anyone before. And would I swear to God I wouldn't tell. I swore. He began to talk about the Brothers 'way back then'. His tone got terser and terser as he got closer to the ugly rat in his soul.

'They liked my bottom, Henry. They did things to me.'

First of all I felt hatred, then envy. That his sin was mild enough to be disclosed. I felt the shadow of Hilbig move through me—his boots, his tongue, his chipped front tooth, the dangling thing, his broad leather hand that moved like sandpaper over your skin, the thump of his truncheon on your back, his whip on your bottom, his fat heavy breath that smelled of egg, the boom and the splinter of a war that did not end until I was born again as Henry in the foothills of the Wicklow mountains. I was damned if I was going to tell Oliver who I was, what I had done. He was too good a friend to lose. I left him with his Christian Brothers by the canal. Dear Oliver, you had nothing to be ashamed of. The world's more full of weeping than you could ever understand. I'll never tell you how I got this wooden leg. I'll never tell you what happened.

The week the Russians liberated Kiev, my mother took me out to the snow and told me, under a bony apple tree, that I was to be friendly to them if they came our way.

'They'll be smiling as they advance, Henryk. They'll smile as they pillage and rape. We'll have to smile and run.'

When I came in with the wood that day, I saw Hilbig at the top of the stairs in his dressing gown. He stood there, with his raised hand shaking, groping for the pomp that he had lost since we first met. He was by now a seasoned addict of Ukrainian vodka.

'Heinrich!'

I stopped dead.

'Do you know that the Führer is going to win this war?'

'Yes, Herr Oberscharführer.'

'I am going to burn the forest down until there's nothing left but charred trees and burnt flesh. I will do it for my Führer.'

He turned and climbed the stairs with a stoop that betrayed the conviction of what he'd said. His dressing gown trailed behind him like a shed skin. Poor, punctured Hilbig was shrivelling up. There were no more lessons in the schoolroom. He knew they'd lost the war.

It was I who had to tell him the vodka source was drying up. There were not enough potatoes to distil even the crudest beverage for old Hilbig. He chased me around the house with a gleaming knife, screaming *Schweinhund! Schweinhund!*, growling when he stopped to rest and pant.

'You sold it to the Russians, you little bastard!'

He chased me outside into the snow, waving his knife over his head. I waded through the snow to the orchard wall. As he lunged at me I leapt aside and he caught my foot. The alligator had got me. The jaws sank in. I could not see what was happening. My face was buried in a drift of snow but I felt the knife against my toe. I prayed to God. I clenched my teeth. The cut was swift and smooth; the agonizing pain came after. I had lost my right big toe. Hilbig bounded about in the orchard with my toe in his hand, playing with it as cats do with half-dead mice.

He flung it into the air hollering *Eins-zwei-drei!* with glee, and caught it as it fell. He did it again and again until it disappeared forever into the snow. Hilbig went back into the house like a child that has become bored and exasperated with its toy. I pulled myself out of the snow and looked at my foot: there, in place of my toe, was a bleeding stump. A deep red patch stained the snow around it. I screamed myself to sleep and woke up a day later with a bandaged foot and my mother at my side. Hilbig allowed me extra meat for a week. I needed iron, he said, to replace the blood. As if someone else had done it.

Hilbig went into decline with a lot of noise. Before the summer of our liberation we saw him dance like Lear around the orchards singing what we suspected were not Odes to the Führer. In the evenings he would prowl about the house with the bearskin on his back, alternating between song and feigned regal pomp. He brought my mother under the bearskin with him, and told her that he had seen furniture made from human bones, lampshades made from human skin, mattresses stuffed with human hair. My mother did not understand. She thought he was talking about the craftwork of a primitive African tribe.

I don't suppose there is a Jew left in Lvov. Those that the Einsatzgruppe and men like Hilbig did not raze down in the Jewish cemetery were sent to camps to be 'resettled' forever. I remember once going to Lvov on market day with my mother and Stanislav, before the war. It was raining that day, and we left the market with our coats over our heads, making for the Jewish Quarter where the old tailor lived. I don't remember his name. His wife baked sumptuous pastries. He always gave us some when we came with our mother to collect our clothes. You could see him sitting at his window. He wore a cap and a long, whitening beard.

As he sewed he made wide, sweeping movements with his long arm and his absurdly long thread. He was more like an orchestral conductor than a little Jewish tailor in Lvov. He played music on a gramophone that had a large horn. *Für Elise*. I remember that. He would grin and smile at us from his open window. Our mother would scold us for eating too many pastries. He would always say: 'Ach … leave the boys. I am fast eater. I vas all der time. I vas when vas yung boy at home I vas fast, fast, fast. I vork fast, but now I slow down. Eat, boys, eat!'

His wife would fuss about us, ruffling our hair as we gulped down pastry after divine pastry.

'Ach schveetheart, Mamushka, leave the boys, day jus fast eaters like me.'

I wonder was he shot or gassed. If he was gassed, was it with Zyklon B or the fumes of an old diesel tank? Ach, I don't know. The man is gone, his wife is gone, their children are gone, their parents are gone, every kin they ever had and every neighbour they ever had is gone. Maybe one of his needles survived in the slit between his wooden floorboards. If it did, it was a lucky needle. Goodbye, Mr Schveetheart Tailor, Goodbye Mrs Schveetheart Tailor! Goodbye all of you who left the world through the chimneys of crematoria. Ollie, you thought you suffered. As the wise old Jew said, it's all relative. I praise what is truly alive, what longs to be burnt to death. Goethe. Goodnight.

4

My short-term memory is abysmal. It has always been like that. When I was twenty or so I took my stepfather's Morris Minor for a jaunt and left it parked on Merrion Square. I came back a few hours later to find the steering wheel had been removed. Now who the hell, I thought, would bother to run off with the steering wheel and leave the car behind? In those days one did not have to lock one's vehicle. What a foolish crook! I thought. I was amusing myself with the thought of him driving his invisible car with glee along the streets, when someone came up behind me and tapped my shoulder.

'Excuse me.'

An American female was at my back.

'That's my car you're peering into.'

And so it was. Not the right car at all. Hers was a blue left-hand-drive car. Mine was a red right-hand-drive parked around the corner on a double yellow line. I tore up my parking ticket and took the girl to lunch. You see, it always works out in the end. What a gallant young man I was.

As soon as I am introduced to someone, I forget their name. As soon as I am given directions, I forget which way to go. Numbers lose their sequence the very second they are dictated to me. I frequently forget my own telephone number and have never mastered any of my friends', never mind those of my colleagues.

But the Hilbig years cling to me with appalling tenacity. Oh, I keep them at bay most of the time. But some brazen object or phrase or a deceitful little dream at night will activate my secret with servile verisimilitude. The shame of what happened. The utter shame. Here we go round, here we go round, here we go round the merry go round. Over and over and over again. If there is one person to whom I have been loyal in this life it has been my mother. She made me promise never to tell what I saw and what I heard in sunny wartime Poland. If anybody asked, we spent the war in one of Stalin's Siberian death factories. But nobody ever did ask. People didn't seem to be bothered by the war in these parts. Except for those who happened to be on the North Strand the night the Germans dropped a bomb by accident.

People, friends I mean, have been alarmed by the announcement of my trip to Poland. What would you want to go there for, Henry? Beetroots and the Pope and Ballymun landscape. I was born there, I say. You were what? Born there? How did you get to be born there? Well I knew you had a bit of German in you, but I didn't know about this at all. Where did you say it was you were born? Lvov, I tell them. Where's that? Just beside Poland, I say. I am Polish. My father was Polish and my mother was Polish and I am going back to Poland to visit my Polish brother after fifty years. So where did you get your German, Henry? Trinity College, I tell them, with utter conviction.

The other night I walked into Doheny's and Arthur pokes his head out of the snug to holler, 'Here's our Russian refugee! How's Gorbachev keeping, Foley?'

I had, in my more recent past, a reputation for being of German extraction. In my early days at school I used to come home and cry for Hilbig. My shoddy short-term memory was even then at work. I remembered singing Schubert on the knee of my surrogate, racially superior father. My mother walloped me black for harping on about Hilbig, but that was too meagre an exorcism to get him out. He has been with me to this very day.

In May 1944, we got a message from Tomasz, the Home Army soldier who had brought my brother to Kraków days after the Germans had captured us. Hilbig was on the Russian front counter-offensive on the river Dniester, south of Lvov. One of

Hilbig's dissident officers slipped the note under the door of our cellar room, where we were habitually locked up. The key to the cellar was wrapped up in the note. We were all against the Russians now. We were to be in the orchard at three that morning, and from there Tomasz would take us back to old Jozef's farm. The dissident officer would lead us out. Tomasz shook our hands under the apple trees in silence, and, creeping slowly through the woods, we left our home for good. I was terrified of what beasts might find us there. What if Hilbig, in his steaming madness, decided he would burn the forest down after all? This was how the war would end ... we would gallop into the forest and never be found again. We would die with Eliot's whimper on our frost-bitten lips and rot with the leaves on the forest floor.

The Führer was not dead yet but belief in him was dying. Hilbig had given up by then. I pitied him, having to be out along the Dniester, fighting Russians. He would have to flee. But how would he leave without his little collection of Volksdeutsche? I thought of him, with his big red face and his paunch. I thought how hurt he'd be that we'd left without him, in the middle of the night. We didn't even leave a thank-you note for all he'd done. Hilbig loved us, I know he did. And I loved Hilbig. Mama, Mama, shouldn't we at least say goodbye? Tomasz snarled at me in the dark, like one of Papa's beasts.

Jozef's house was full of partisans. They all poured out of the barn when they saw us in the distance, releasing the safety-catches on their rifles, spitting out pellets of phlegm. Jozef did not come out to greet us. He was dead, and so was his wife. Nobody could tell us why. Tomasz bundled us in and said we could sleep till dark, and then we'd have to leave and travel through the night. He told Mama, over pale dead borsch, that he knew where Papa was. Mama looked up, and pushed her bowl in front of her. He knew where Papa was? Papa is in England, said Tomasz, and I can bring you there.

'To England?' Mama said.

'To England.'

'But what about Stanislav?' she said.

'For all you know he might be dead. Anyway, there's no time to go to Kraków. We have to leave for the mountains tonight. We have to get out of here before the Russians come. Once they cross the Vistula, Poland has fallen.'

I sneaked into the barn before we left that night, and found no trace of our paintings, nor Papa's rococo clock. Only stolen cans of petrol and rifles.

Over the next six months we lived in the wilds of the Tatra Mountains, with the Red Army on either side of us in Poland and in Czechoslovakia. Our bed was the forest floor, our food the animals that Tomasz snared, the roots of plants, and whatever we could beg from peasants. In the winter, we were lucky. Some peasants took us in. If not for that, Mama would have died, so severe were her frostbite and her pulmonary condition. My leg was battered, and my hands were covered in warts and raw blisters from the sticks I'd used as crutches.

We were hidden in the loft of a little wooden house on a slope so steep I thought the house would tumble down it in the middle of the night. Especially since our hosts were so very large. How they had kept that blubber throughout the war I do not know. But they seemed, in their brightly painted wooden house, utterly oblivious to the war. They were the sort of rosy-cheeked, mildly deranged people you would expect mountain folk to be. I think they cried when we left. They gave us a horse and cart. I can remember them waving to us from the doorway of their home, framed by bright blue and yellow slats of wood. I would never see them again. We were on the road and the war was nearly over. Hurrah! We were going to England to find Papa and Big Ben.

The sun poured down all over us and made the snow-capped mountains look immaculate. Somewhere in the town of Zakopane I smelt pancakes, but I never found them. My empty stomach moaned for them all the way up the river Oder, where we travelled. I shall always regret not finding those pancakes.

By the time we got to the German border, houses were up in flames everywhere. Charred black bodies hung out of the tops of German tanks. Frozen dead children were being carried along the roads in sheets. German refugees were tearing over the border in their thousands. We pretended to be German. Tomasz was only delighted, I saw then, to be with Volksdeutsche. He took charge of our Ahnentafel, in case we were asked for papers.

By the time Berlin had fallen, we were already in Cham Transient Displaced Persons camp in Germany, where we stayed for another six months. After being deloused we were issued six tins of sardines and a loaf of bread. As the second last sardine slithered down my throat a boy with plump cheeks and golden hair asked me for a sardine.

'I've finished.'

'Give me some of your bread. I'm starving. Listen to my stomach.'

Indeed, it howled. But I was not about to give a plump little German-speaking boy my last sardine. The place was crawling with little Volksdeutsche children. These little dears, after being examined by 'Racial Science Experts', had been taken in by German foster parents. Now the Child Tracing Team was sending them back to Poland where they belonged. I felt like a scrawny hen in a sty full of well fed pigs. How did he dare to ask me for my last sardine when he had been gorging on strudel for the whole of the war? There was a soft, bloated look in his eyes. I had black circles around my eyes and cold sores on my lips. And I had lost my toe. I called him a Nazi pig and he trotted off obediently.

5

I swore to keep my mouth shut. Bloody secrets. As a rule I don't keep other people's secrets, because I have been forced to lock my truth away for all this time. Nobody understands that, of course. People don't like my busy tongue. But by telling other people's secrets I am led away from the temptation to tell my own. Dear old Mumsy, I may have been a rotten little Catholic, but I kept my word. Nobody can call us collaborators. Hilbig is dead and we are admitting nothing.

When we were finally released from the D.P. camp, we took a train to Paris from Frankfurt. Tomasz had pulled a wad of notes out of his jacket lining. He'd stolen the money from Hilbig's office the night we'd left Lvov. My mother did not approve, but she promised that we would have ice cream in Paris, in any case. When we got to Paris, there was none. We ate baguettes on the corners of sweeping boulevards and slept in the Luxembourg Gardens.

Three weeks later we took the boat at Dieppe. There it was: the sea! A thing I had never seen before. Liquid sky. Navy, silver, green by the time we got to Newhaven and the sun was climbing down the sky and grey clouds came rushing in from the west to greet us. Wind heaved against us, rain spat. We squinted and frowned at this inhospitality.

Exhausted, we took a train to London. Tomasz spent weeks with us at the Red Cross trying to trace Papa. Finally we met a Polish RAF pilot who did not know Papa, but advised us to go to Bournemouth, where several Polish families had already settled, who might take us in. Mama was not convinced. She told Tomasz to go ahead, we would follow later.

But we never followed Tomasz down to Bournemouth. We had come to Victoria Station to buy our tickets and poor Mummy was so tired and hungry that she got a little flustered—was it Victoria or Paddington she should be in? She stopped a man in a green overcoat, by the ticket booth. He turned around and smiled and his dimples creased. I knew we had found a friend.

'To Bournemouth?' my mother said.

'Burn mouth? I beg your pardon?' the man in the overcoat said, and his dimples creased again, and he slurped in saliva from the insides of his cheeks.

'Nikolai!' exclaimed my mother. He scratched the back of his neck, and stole a quick glance at the mother and child. He saw the hunger gnawing at us, he saw our little cardboard boxes tied with string, full of nothing.

'Well, I'm not Nicholas. But these are hard times. Can I get you a cup of tea?' My mother and I stood there, silent. The sun poured in and warmed the tiles of Victoria Station. The man with the dimples had done this. We followed him to the tea-stall and sat with him on a bench. He handed us each a cup of tea.

'My name is Liam,' he said, and shook my mother's rigid

hand. 'I'm looking for my English cousin. Where is it you're from?'

'Po-land,' I said. 'My Mama can speak German. Not English.' Liam's eyebrows leapt up his forehead and fell down again. He slurped up his saliva, and broke into fluent German with an Irish accent. 'Now, who the hell is Nikolai?' he parped. Nikolai was a professor from Lvov University: the same green overcoat, the same friendly smile. And Liam comes back at her with the tale of his lost cousin, Bernadette, who had been a nurse in a German D.P. camp, who, would you believe it, looked not unlike my mother: the same eyes, and the hair, but yours is lighter.

Liam Driscoll, the charming old fox. He took us to the Victoria café, and got us marrowfat peas and sausages with his food coupons, and proceeded, as he squashed his peas with the back of his fork, to tell my mother all about the little island he was from. My mother ate slowly, pea by precious pea. She still thought they were Nikolai's dimples, and that was Nikolai's coat, hanging on the back of the chair. She would have married Nikolai if he had not run away to Cracow with her sister. She would have married Nikolai if he had not left her sister for a Jewish girl from Kazimierz. Mama never mentioned that we were searching for my Papa. (Later, in the public toilets, she pinched me on the arm and told me not to say a word about my father.) I'll tell you one thing about the Emergency, Liam said, I was never short of food. You don't need to be bothered with this coupon business over there. And my mother looked up from her plate, which had three peas left on it, and a morsel of sausage gristle. You mean, there's plenty of food over there? asked my mother. And ice cream? I asked. Barrelfuls, said Liam. We were persuaded: we would go to Ireland on the boat. Don't you worry, said Liam, I'll organize it all.

I'll get on to Joe, and he'll meet you at the boat. And another thing—I've a friend of a friend who knows the Polish Ambassador. Dobrzynski—is that his name?

The next day we took the mailboat to Ireland. A vast, leaking plateau of grey descended, and followed us across the water. Mother stood with her back to Ireland for the whole crossing, wishing Nikolai had come. That was Mumsy: always looking back. He'd kissed her cheek when we were getting on the boat. She'd pressed his podgy hand, and said goodbye to her Nikolai. Well, things would be different now.

A plump man in a tweed jacket met us at the mailboat pier in Dun Laoghaire. Two very ill, pale green refugees we were for we had vomited our way over a sea tormented by a force-ten gale. When Joe O'Donnell shook my hand he squashed my brittle knuckles as if he wished to crush them. I could not be convinced that this was hospitality. I gasped with pain. I couldn't help it. But Joe O'Donnell didn't notice. We were friends of Liam Driscoll's and that was all he needed to know. He linked arms with my mother and launched into jolly gung-ho German. He introduced us to his shiny black Ford Model V-8 with a broad, proud sweep of his arm. You are very welcome, he said, and we embarked. Where are we, Mummy? Why do they speak German in Ireland? Why is it winter here already? My foot is sore and I am hungry. I have been hungry for six years. Be quiet Henry. Stop complaining. It is rude.

Joe did not know where we had come from, what régime our Oberscharführer had had us under. To him, we were a pair of war-weary Polish refugees bestowed on him by an old friend. Joe, our saviour. Our cheery, tweed-clad German-speaking saviour who tucked us into his war-free zone as if we were his own.

We learned later that he had owed Liam a favour. Joe, who ranked high in the old IRA but not as high as Liam, had made a right old shambles of their sabotage plan against England in 1939. In cahoots with the Abwehr, he'd made the most hazardous grenades any man had ever used, and had blown his own fingers off at the first demonstration. A bunch of IRA men were found mutilated under their own bicycles after Joe's ramshackle grenades had exploded when they plunged into giant English potholes. The rest were arrested. God love them. What a feat of incompetence. I believe Joe was fiercely ashamed of this fiasco. He'd lived in fear of Liam ever since. When we met Liam, he was looking for men that had been lost since 1939. We would never see Liam 'Nikolai' Driscoll again. There was no Bernadette, and there was a warrant out for his arrest.

We told Joe about Siberia and nothing else. From Siberia to the Sally Gap! Well here you are now, Joe said, this is Ireland and you're lucky you're not Jewish or you'd never have got in. Dev put a ban on that class of refugee, you see. I remember when Joe's wife opened the door to us, so proud of her newly whitewashed farmhouse. Things seemed so solid here, so unshakeably and stubbornly solid. When she saw us she took a step back in shock and knocked her head against a hanging geranium. It swung back and forth, like a pendulum.

'Mother of God, Joe. They're half dead.'

We were torn and stained and very thin, but I had seen skeletons walking on the roads back there. Mrs O'Donnell was looking at a pair of well-fed refugees.

'Come in, come in, and have a cup of tea,' she croaked.

Her big bosom pressed against me as she ushered us into her greasy abode. She brought us tea in a giant red pot. Laughter.

Tea. Laughter. Laugh, laugh, laugh. My mother smiled stiffly in the corner clutching the teacup-thin fingers. She had once been so good at this. The only familiar thing was the clock ticking dependably in the hall beyond the racket of our hollering hosts.

6

Poor old Stan, poor old Stan. What would become of him, I wondered. My mother wept and sent letter after letter imploring him to join us in Ireland. I presume, since Stanislav never came, that the aunt devoured the correspondence. Time passed. I regret to say I forgot about old Stan, or at least stopped wondering about him. After a few months in the O'Donnells', I became the plump, garrulous Henry that I am today. While my mother spent the summer in Dublin, where she was working at the Shelbourne Hotel, I stayed at the farm tormenting the cats, gobbling fruit from the trees and mastering the Irish-English tongue at breakneck speed.

I claimed my right to be Irish by becoming a veritable addict of tea and stout. I lay the blame for my addiction to the latter on Madame O'Donnell, who, after the first rite of initiation in the back room, declared that this black slop would 'build me up'. It sent me into a delirious fog, out of which Hilbig and his Doberman friends emerged. I staggered around the farmhouse while Mrs O'Donnell held her sides in glee as she watched alcohol triumph over what she thought was innocence. I would bump into things and burp and launch into an incomprehensible gibberish that combined Hilbig words with Hiberno-English.

'Dirty-looking Schweinhund ... schmutzige-hic-eedeeot! Wo

ist meine Mutti? Vers my motter und Hilbig? Ver-hic-wo ist Herr Oberscharführer?'

'What did ye say Henry? That's a good one. Say it again. Go on!'

Mrs O'Donnell had never seen anything so funny in her life. Thank God she couldn't understand me. It was therapeutic, I suppose. Saying what I'd wanted to say to Hilbig after all those years, yelling my guts raw out into the open yard where the chickens stared bewildered and aslant. He still had a livid eye on me, even then. And I still missed him, and felt sorry that we'd left him alone. I still wondered what he did when he came back to the manor and found us gone. If he ever came back from the Dniester, that is. His good son Heinrich was still waiting for him to bring us back to the Fatherland.

My mother came back at the end of the summer in a pale blue gabardine coat. She looked pious and withdrawn, at a raw kind of peace with herself. When she saw her beer-bellied, limping ten-year-old child, she knew there was something wrong.

'What has happened to you, Henryk? You look fat and sick.'

Mrs O'Donnell was in the kitchen trying to appear engrossed in her invented task. Pots banged and taps were turned but I knew by now how well tuned were her ears. I whispered to my mother: 'Mama, I can feel my toe even though it's not there. The one that Hilbig took, I mean.'

'Don't speak of that fiend, Henryk. Show me.'

I peeled off my sock and revealed a shrivelled, black foot. Hilbig's masterpiece. My mother went pale. I had begun to rot. Mr O'Donnell took me to the hospital that afternoon in his Ford Model V-8. I lay on the back seat looking out beyond my mutant foot to green hills soaring gently into a band of blue. I was in treacherous pain: I needed a father.

A starched angelic nurse in the hospital told me everything was going to be all right. I could see little black hairs up her nostrils when she leaned over me. Not so angelic after all. When she asked me how I lost my toe I told her a wild Polish wolf had bitten it off in the woods one day when I got lost in the forest behind my house. She laughed and stuck a needle into my arm and made me pee into a glass phial. I had not expected to be tortured. They found Mrs O'Donnell's black medicine in my urine and expressed grave concern to my wheezing mother. Her lungs had never recovered from that evening with Hilbig.

They put me out with ether and set about dismantling my leg. Dry gangrene had blocked my arteries. There was nothing for it but the chop. Off with his leg! Off with his poisoned little limb! The doctor, a grizzly Northern Irish goat, showed me the designs for my new leg with an insidious and curious glint in his eye.

'We'll give you a wee wooden one that'll fit just the same. Don't you worry abite a thing, mister.'

Don't worry about a thing, you hoary old Frankenstein! You stole my leg. I was but ten years old, a seasoned drinker, and a crippled, weary veteran of war. The bastards never even asked me. I don't suppose my mother could have faced forewarning me of what my leg was destined for. Better to let him wake up in the morning with half his leg chopped off. Then there'll be nothing he can do about it. I stayed in the hospital for two weeks. By night Hilbig chased me with a hatchet, by day my invisible limb raged with a cursed, pointless itch.

The leg does not detract. It might be different if I was a woman. But as a man with a wooden leg I fancy I look windswept and heroic. I've told so many tales about it. It's not the only odd thing about Henry. I used to disappear for weeks into the woods to stay with Mumsy and the Step, when things got bad. When the world began to slant at a gruesome, unsettling angle. I get these unpleasant attacks. It is I that am aslant, of course, and not the world. I get out of kilter. I cease to hear what people say, I cease to believe what I see in front of me. I walk lopsided. I lose my speech. My eyes dilate and my mouth becomes dry. I retreat to my mother in the woods. I lie low and horizontal and think of death. It is an existential, and not a chemical disorder. Regardless, they have locked me up more times than I care to record.

Sometimes these attacks last for months. But there is an advantage to them. Nobody knows where I have gone. Some think that I have taken my body to foreign parts. I let them believe it. I spin glorious narratives for them about volunteering in the Afghan War, meditating in Ladakhi monasteries, guzzling absinthe in the south of Spain. The women who know me less well tend to believe me. The rest of them throw their eyes heavenward and snidely warn me to take my medication. They're only stories. Harmless stories. Why should I tell them where I've really been? Why should I tell them that I have been wrapped in the foetal position with a damp dressing gown stuck to my skin, that I have been numb with the moronic tranquillizers of the psychiatric trade and hoarse with the groaning that my pain evokes? To hell with the public! This is Henry. There is a time-honoured tradition of yarn-spinning in Henry's world. Fiction is my antidote. About my leg, I told them that I met a Russian partisan in the woods one day in the war. He shot off my leg and roasted it on a spit before my very eyes. Forgive me. I know I'm foolish. But it raised a few plucked eyebrows.

Imagine that with all those shrinks poking at my sores, with all the dope they had me consume, I never said a word about Hilbig, about what happened. Would they have had a remedy for my dear old Oberscharführer? Of course not. Nobody on this mossy little island would ever understand. Not even Mr O'Donnell, who had a few Nazi pals drop in on him by parachute from Heinkel III bombers in the summer of 1940. They hid in Joe's safehouse in the Wicklow hills, camouflaged behind the apple trees. When they went off to meet the IRA Chief of Staff, they were snared, swallowed their cyanide pills and were buried in Glencree's purpose-built German Cemetery. Joe took a while to live that one down. It was another thing that Liam Driscoll would never forgive him for.

Nobody can understand this Henry who hobbles about the streets of Dublin with rings on his fingers and bolts on his dear old toes. Nobody knows where I came from and nobody knows where I am going. Those people are my friends. We toddle about under the same grey sky and grind our feet into the same ground. Friends. Close. Yet very far apart.

7

My mother abandoned me to a National School on the other side of the valley. This odd, cornflower-eyed, thick-fringed Nazi-educated cripple was mocked like a child was never mocked at school. I was a Nazi, a Jew, a gypsy and a poshboy all in one. I was utterly confused. I exchanged my Polish-German accent for their hard Wicklow tones. I hid my face in the leaves of old, weathered books. I had a firm grip on Greek, Latin and English, and I had a smattering of Irish by the time I was sent to boarding school for my secondary education. What an ugly, but polyglot, little duckling I was then.

We stayed with the O'Donnells for my primary school years. My mother worked in Dublin during the week. We became accustomed to the sullen, indistinguishable Irish seasons. A few days of snow in winter, a few days of sun in summer, and the rest a low, bland stretch of grey. None of the high majestic skies of Lvov summers. My mother learned to communicate in English. Polish was no longer spoken between us. It was the language of our Sovietized home, her dead husband, and her lost son. She had become quite odd. I came home from school one day and found her scraping her nails against the walls, sobbing as only she could sob. Mr and Mrs O'Donnell had gone to Dublin for the day. When she had dried up she came over to me with a glazed look in her eyes. She said in a rather sinister tone that she had something to show me. We sat by the open fire. She took a bulging envelope out of her bag. Her hands were shaking. She tore away the envelope and there, in her hand, was a finger bone with a golden ring around it.

'Henry, this is your father's finger. I have found him in Belfast.'

Poor, sweet, deranged mother. Henry, is there a history of madness in your family? No, God no, I'm the only one. God forbid, isn't one enough? You see, mother, I guarded your insanity like the crown jewels. Had I not, I might have saved my own skin. They might have been able to sort me out without stuffing me up to the eyelids with drugs that would have horrified Dean Swift. For all I know, our whole lineage might have been barking mad. I'll never know. My mother refused to speak of anything that preceded 1945. But I can vouch for my mother's madness. I don't know if it was genes or the war that sent her mad. So how normal can I be, with a mother that brought home bones she claimed were from my father's hand? I admit, there is a possibility that her story was true, that somehow we had in fact found our way to the very land in which her dead husband lay. I do remember a very gaunt Polish man visiting my mother, running his long finger over a map of Belfast. He was an RAF pilot, so that would fit. I believe he told her that Papa had choked on a fish bone in a Belfast chipper. They had been stationed there just after the Battle of Britain. He wouldn't have been used to fish, of course, being from landlocked Lvov.

It's a wonder anyone ever wanted to marry my poor mother again. If Eddy Foley had not come along when he did my mother might have brought the whole skeleton home with her, and propped it up in bed beside her. Eddy did not come along as such. He sidled up to her, divil that he was. He took months to do it. He skulked around O'Donnells', pretending to look for things in sheds and cupboards when he knew exactly where she was. His great flaw is his hesitancy. His unwillingness to plunge. This is where we differ. He was a columnist, not a journalist. A researcher, not a titillator. So he always said. He had the solid bones my mother needed. Finally, one day, instead of nodding past her in the yard or grunting at her in the corridor, he took her to the orchards and talked to her. I stayed in my room carving pictures on my wooden leg. She came back blushing, and told me we were going to move.

Eddy had built a house in the woods. It was an odd house. He had collected fragments of abandoned buildings and assembled them to his own quirky taste. The bay windows were striking: vast, latticed, pointed things.

'Such nice windows, Mister Foley,' my mother said.

'Thank you, Elizabeth. I got them from an old Protestant church up the road.'

My mother laughed coquettishly and, behind him, clasped the cross around her neck. I think she was afraid to step inside. We paused in the garden before the house took us in through its warped, crooked door. This was to be our home. I eyed it with suspicion. Inside, it was cold. It was a stone-built open-plan house undecorated but for Eddy's thousands-strong army of books that lined the walls.

Eddy drove us to mass that evening in the local village. My weeping mother pressed her head against the pew, rubbing that foul bone with the ring on it, atoning, I suppose, for having already found her second man. Old women stole glances at her from under their scarves. They nodded conspiratorially to the peculiarity their parish had acquired. When mass was over they shuffled down the aisles in droves, whispering shamelessly to each other.

Would you look at that one crying her eyes out over there Maisy that's the one with the accent you know Foley's going to marry a foreigner would you believe would you look at the cheekbones on her I bet she's a communist from Russia.

She was never accepted. She was met by a hush in every local shop. Everywhere she went she was met with this tepid, unsettling silence. They were always about to pounce, and never did. There were rumours about her. Mr Foley would have his regrets, they said. You just wait and see. It always goes wrong with those foreigners.

The trouble was, they were right.

Across the field, pitched on the summit of a green slope, there stood a large ochre house. It was not like our house, which was all hunched up in the woods. It proclaimed itself from the top of the hill with pride and confidence. I was not allowed to pry. I was to wait, politely, for an invitation. But how were they to know of my existence if I didn't declare myself to them at their door? I clambered through the fields, waded up the stream and hauled my wooden leg up the hill to the giant wooden door that I had seen from the window of my sparse, damp little room. I pressed my two thumbs against a bell set in the fluting of the doorjamb. Nobody answered. The wind rushed against the windows. Filthy windows with cobwebs encrusted on the inside. An oval hunting table stood like a flat-backed beast in the middle of the dining room. Cold, supercilious women stared down at me from gilded frames. Not an animate object in sight. I looked in the gable window at a torn sofa, Louis Quinze chairs with the paint peeling off in layers as thin as the skin that peels away from birch trees. I found the air of decay comforting. Around the back, down a slope I found a walled garden guarding nothing but a tangle of weeds and hostile brambles. A pair of plaster Grecian urns sat smugly behind a matted trellis.

I heard a car crack the gravel on the drive. I ran back to the front door. Can you imagine me standing there, a crippled boy of twelve with a pudding-bowl haircut, a plump little face with a snotty nose stuck on it and his sock pulled over his misshapen wooden leg, grinning from ear to ear, inanely eager to please? Dr Clive Hawkins got out of his car and stared in disbelief.

'Who the devil are you?'

'Good afternoon, sir. I-am-coming-to-visit.'

'You're what? Who the hell are you?'

'I am Henry Malinski, sir.'

'You'll have to get off my land before I have you—'

'I'm only came to visit, sir. I live with my mother over there—'

Mrs Hawkins threw her head back and let out peals of laughter. She slammed the car door shut to show that she had finished. Mirren: always dramatic. She held out her hand to me.

'Clive, let the little boy come in and have some tea.'

She led me down the hall of Holly Park. Everything was warped. The wallpaper bulged with pockets of damp; the portraits undulated and could not see straight out of the windows. The Georgian glass smeared imperfection on the outside world. I was given a glass of milk and biscuits in the drawing room. Mrs Hawkins sat opposite me with her hands folded over her middle and had a good, long look at me. I was embarrassed to have her hear me crunching like a puppy on the biscuits.

'Henry, you must tell me where you're from.'

I pointed across the field.

'Originally, I mean.'

'Poland, madame.'

'Poland! And why are you here, Henry?'

'The war, madame.'

'But it's over!'

'The Russians.'

'Oh, I see.'

'Madame, are you baroness?'

'Me? Goodness no. Oh, the portraits, yes. Not my relatives, Henry. Nor Dr Hawkins'. We bought the house with everything in it. More milk, Henry?'

'Yes, please. Very good milk here, madame.'

'Thank you, Henry.'

'Does Mister Hawkins hunt in forest?'

'The forest, Henry. Goodness no. Hasn't got the time.'

'Are there wolves in the forest, madame, and wild pigs?'

'There is not an animal in Ireland that will harm you, Henry. Saint Patrick sent them all off on a boat to England. But Henry—hunting is not kind. Animals have rights too. Dr Hawkins' father was a very good vet, you know. A pioneer of animal rights.'

'I am sorry?'

'People shouldn't kill animals, Henry. I don't know what they do out there in Poland or Russia … but it isn't right, you know.'

'No madame, it isn't right.'

If she only knew what my father had shot in the forest. If she could just see the dislocated heads of bear, pig and deer grafted to the walls of our home. And the birds of Lvov stuffed dry and plump. I did not come from a world of animal rights. But then, neither did Mrs Hawkins. When the bugle sounded over Donnymead Hill, she would gallop to the bottom of the garden and scream at them to get off her land: but on the redcoats thundered, like the pictures that you see on place-mats.

Dr Hawkins was curious about my leg. I was an interesting specimen to this man. He gave me physiotherapy on the lawn when he had time. Mrs Hawkins drilled me in the drawing room on Thursday afternoons: *the*, Henry. Use that definite article where it is required. Dr Hawkins came to our house one evening and asked my mother about my leg. Where had it come from?

'That hospital in Bray. They got it from the north of Ireland.'

'But why—the operation?'

'Was infection, Mister Hawkins. Very bad infection.'

'From what?'

'Some cut he had—'

'What cut?'

'The toe.'

'Which toe?'

'One of the toes, Mister Hawkins. One of the toes. I cannot tell you which toe.'

'Why not?'

'Because I do not know.'

By the time I had mastered the use of the definite article in English, Tristan Hawkins had come home from boarding school. At first he had been offended by this foreign deformity that his mother urged him to befriend. Slowly, he gave way to my daily visits. We became partners in vandalism. One day, with the sun beating uncharacteristically down on our backs, we built a house of haystacks in the field. Triss went off to get a candle. It was dark inside our house of straw. Back he came with a fistful of candles and a box of matches. The first match sent sixty acres of golden hay into orange flame. All that was left was a scorched black patch of earth. Though it was clearly Tristan's fault, Dr Hawkins decided I had had a perilous effect on his son. He barred me from the house. But I would steal across the fields at night, and we would prowl around the cellars, in candlelight, hazardously drunk on family gin.

I hated my boarding school. I hid myself and my contraption in the library for the first year. My peers were superstitious: I must have done something rotten to deserve a wooden leg. The teachers shared this attitude. But I won them over with my dazzling aptitude for every subject on the school curriculum. They had me converted from writing with my left hand to my right, from Catholicism to the Church of Ireland. I joined the choir. I began to feel roused by those solemn gems of the *Church Hymnal*: 'Onward Christian Soldiers' and 'Abide With Me'. To my mother's horror, I felt at home with these Anglophile melodies.

She tried to blame the Hawkinses, she tried to blame my father. She tried to get me out of the school. But I would not leave. I had social ladders to climb and many, many more bridges to burn.

By the time I left school I had become an irreverent sweaty-palmed young man with a middle-class Dublin accent and a brilliant turn of phrase. I remember how I hated coming home. My mother was always sitting on the same shabby chair, folded up like a little bird, prim and disapproving. We did not speak of the past. We stared at each other, uncomprehending, from the opposite ends of rooms. She shuddered when I told her I intended to read German at university.

'I prefer you study Russian than that tongue.'

It was as if I had invited Hilbig to tea.

'You really want to study that language?'

I nodded, with cordial menace. There was no more understanding between us. I waved to her through the latticed window as I was leaving. She stood there, looking down at me, but did not raise her hand. The last tangible piece of Lvov was disappearing down the lane. The trees groaned in the wind. I did not look back again but I felt her eyes on my back all the way to the end of the lane.

8

I was now free to roam the broad and narrow streets of Dublin. My stepfather made my university studies possible. He generously donated part of his dead mother's well-hoarded dowry to my cause. Good old Step. As far as he was concerned we were all destined for the boat. I might as well bring a good education with me. His daughter Siobhán, still a stranger to me, had left for London ten years ago.

Oh, la! I remember that eruption of youthful hope, as I stood with my legs apart outside the gates of Trinity College, between the statues of Oliver Goldsmith and Edmund Burke. I had my hands in my pockets and a cigarette hanging from my lips. To hell with you, mother, I said, and I breathed in the width and breadth of the College Green panorama. To hell with you, I'm a stray dog now. I felt as sturdy as the House of Lords columns, as valiant as a Dublin bus, as virile as a Kilmainham rabbit.

I remember my first woman. A doe-faced one in Davy Byrne's with bulbous calves and square knees. A country girl from God knows where. I bought her a drink. Henry was going to have a go at fondling the female species. She liked my irreverence. She liked my sandy hair.

'You remind me of a boy I met from Sweden called Sven. Or was it Denmark?'

The parochial innocence, the barefaced lie. The pub became a swirl of warm smoke, sweet booze, tinkling glasses. I was wonderfully, warmly drunk. Sweat dribbled down my temples. Her teeth flashed at me. She coyly slid her finger over her bottom lip. There was no more conversation to be had. It was time to commit our sin. We rose, and Henry hobbled to the door.

'Where's my stick? Did you see my stick?'

'What stick?'

'My stick. I need my stick.'

My wretched leg had got the better of me again. I had to attach myself to the wee doe's neck and have her take me back to my Trinity rooms. I had to ask her to help me up the stairs. She seemed quite keen to help the cripple home. It had been a shock to her to see my broad shoulders so ill-matched by a rickety old leg. I told her the story of the greedy Russian partisan. Go away out of that Henry, she said, and let her head fall to my shoulder. We proceeded to serious matters. I spent the next day with her under the Trinity Campanile, smoking cigarettes and stroking hands. Henry, you're sweet, she said, but I've got to go. She showed me her ticket to Euston, London. Cost her three pounds, one and six. She went off in her wrinkled coat and her laddered stocking. I believe I cried when she'd gone.

I had not chosen to specialize in German to thwart my mother. I chose it because I was fluent and confident in that tongue, which meant I would have less work to do. I would have time to frequent the city's public houses with considerably less guilt.

My drinking took me to strange places. I woke up one morning on Dalkey Island propped against the Martello Tower with a goat peering into my face. I waved to the harbour for attention, but this vertical, one-and-a-half-legged goat attracted nobody's attention; for there was no attention to attract. I stayed on the island for two days nibbling on the leaves of dandelions, chewing cuds of grass. The goats visited me in the tower, offering their droppings to my sorry plight. Finally a little rowing boat appeared on the third day. I waved joyously, jumping from craggy rock to craggy rock. I waved and shouted like a hooligan. The man had jowls and a thick woollen hat. He squinted his eyes and stopped rowing. I stopped waving. It did not seem to be obvious to this man of the sea that this was not where I habitually lived. After his pause, he began to row again in the other direction.

'Hey! Ahoy there! Help!'

He stopped, and rowed over.

'Are you all right there? Is it a lift you want, son?'

'It is!'

He moored himself to one of the craggy rocks and waited for the dishevelled islandman to approach. The gulls surveyed my clumsy exit. I skidded from rock pool to rock pool. The man of the sea held out his salty hand and hauled me on board.

'Thank you, sir, Thank you. Got stuck out there.'

'Ye what?'

'Stuck. Two days. No food. No water.'

'Better get you back to land, so. I thought ye lived in the tower.'

'It's derelict.'

And not another word passed between us. A sharp breeze nudged us back to shore. Hunger assailed me. I begged the Dalkey tram driver to give me a free ride. All right son, he grumbled. I found Oliver in Grogan's and related my tale.

'We were wondering where you'd got to, Henry,' was all he said. Fellows and friends came up to me and gave me back parts of my lost night. How could I forget? they said. They had left me on Dalkey harbour crooning self-piteous serenades to my artificial limb. It was more than a naggin of whiskey, they said. It was a full buxom bottle. You were gazing at the moon, Henry, like a right old pagan. And you were talking about a kraut called Hilbig, or Humbug.

Jesus, holy suffering mother of Divine God, I said to myself. I nearly choked on my smooth black pint. I examined the expression on the faces of my companions. I could detect no malice in them. Oh, ha ha, Hilbig! I said. I'm stuffed to the gills with sauerkraut rant, I said to them. Reading German has that effect. It does, they said, and continued with their banter in the normal manner. I broke out in a cold sweat and began to feel nauseated. But nothing had changed. I was still Henry of the Tall Story. Whatever I said could not be entirely true. Hilbig, you old wolf, you made a Peter of me. They did not even believe my Dalkey Island Adventure. And Thank the Living God for That.

Guilt crept up my thick flannel trousers from the insides of Irish Catholic churches. Thick, Augustinian guilt, egged on from the aisles by my mother. Confess, confess, the voices said. For God's sake! I thought my conversion had exempted me. I had vociferated those Church of Ireland hymns in true and earnest adoration of their neat, hard-working God. I came to you, O Protestants of Ireland, and asked to be purged of the transubstantiationalist rite, the blue frock of the so-called virgin, and the sweaty little box of sins on the aisle. And it had not worked. I still felt I had no right to pray for a healthy limb to stride upon. I still did not deserve. I still felt rotten to the core.

Big, hulking neo-Byzantine churches emerged, as if from underground, all over the city. I cowered as I passed them by. These were the giant, red brick amplifications of my mother's guilt. As she was to be avoided, they were to be avoided. The cold stone of churches. Why so cold? Was there no forgiveness? What if He knew what I had done? I don't just blame my mother for my guilt. It's just that she was always there in the mental space above my ear, mouthing zealously the prayers she thought would save her and never did. Tormented, she was, whether in prayer or out. The war had poured black ink over her vision of life. She could find no way to wash it out. She punished herself instead. Her only pleasure was her garden. She talked to the flowers and, to her credit, enticed some interesting specimens out of the earth. I don't remember the names—were there irises? Yes, there were.

And sweetpeas climbed up a trellis for her one year, but a blast of Irish wind buffeted them down. She grew sunflowers taller than herself one summer. I remember her beaming up at them, extending a finger to stroke the yellow velvet of the petals. She seemed happy then. I'll grant her that. She took me outside to meet the giant flowers.

'Look, Henryk, just like in Lvov. Do you remember fields of these sunflowers behind the house?'

'No, mother, I do not.'

She cowered under her giant flower. I know I shouldn't have. But I couldn't bear to admit that I remembered. That was, I think, my first memory. My mother was holding my hand in the schoolroom. There was light pouring in behind us. Out the window, we could see a vast field full of sunflowers craning their necks to drink in the sun under the sea blue sky. It was very hot, so hot my clothes stuck to me and my mother's palm was clammy. Between the blue and the yellow there flew a stork, straight, along the horizon. It was one of those harmonic moments when one's self dissolves into the surrounding field, and sky, and bird.

But I had to avoid it. I had to avoid her sentimentality. It led one into traps. Like the trap she had led me into the day she was looking for her hats. That could not be forgiven. So I did not give her the pleasure of remembering the sunflowers. I let her wilt with them.

I was always so disappointed when I came home. I thought she would have changed. But she was always that part of me that I could not hack off. The only evidence of my past. None of my friends had met her. I never invited them to the house. I only went back there when I was hungry or broke or in need of a mend.

My stepfather began to confide in me about her, bewildered as he was by her behaviour. We first met as conspirators in the Pearl Bar, opposite the *Irish Times*. It was a gusty afternoon. He told me about an odd thing that had happened recently. Dr and Mrs Hawkins had invited my mother and himself to tea over in Holly Park. Incredibly, my mother consented to go. This was to be her first visit to Holly Park. Eddy said her spirits were gay enough, before they left.

My mother used to glimpse the house through the silver birch trees, over the humpy field. But she had never ventured to it, despite the many invitations. I think she was afraid of Mirren Hawkins' robust, brash attitude to life. It might have knocked my mother down. She was so afraid of everything, the fool. She hid for the whole of her emigrant life.

Dr and Mrs Hawkins greeted them at the door, took their coats, and led them down the hall. My mother surveyed the clocks, rugs, paintings, and furniture with what seemed to my stepfather a covetous eye. The more she looked about the more enraptured she became. She cast a quasi-leer at the silver tea set. She reached out to the teapot, lifted it up and examined its underside, as if to determine its sex. All this time, she did not speak. Her behaviour grew more and more odd as the afternoon progressed. She declined the tea and cake with too much force to be polite. It seemed to Eddy it was the Hawkinses she declined and not their tea. All three felt distinctly ill at ease. It is easy to dismiss a sullen, wordless mouse at tea, but not a skittish Slavic beauty. The more she did not speak, the more she filled the room. An ominous silence took hold of them all. My mother, Elizabeth, as Eddy called her, leapt up from her seat and retreated to the farthest window of the room. She pressed her face against it and gazed out at the silver birches. Eddy coughed and said that, ahem, they'd better be going. Mirren Hawkins ignored him. She got up and joined Elizabeth by the window.

'Henry,' Eddy told me, 'she was crying in the corner like a child.'

Mirren Hawkins put a gawky arm around her shoulder. My mother's tears spilled down and down. She worked herself into a blubbering hysteria, blathering words that no one in the room could understand.

'Be-joe-dja. She said that over and over again. She had her face covered by her hands so it wasn't very clear.'

'Brzoza. Means silver birch. The dwor was surrounded by them.'

'The what?'

'The house we lived in. Dwór. Manor home.'

'Dvoor. She said that too.'

I warned Eddy not to take too much of my mother's nonsense. But he felt guilty. Besides, there was more to that afternoon than a few tears.

Dr Hawkins had made for the door, fumbling for a decent excuse. Mirren and Eddy set about restoring my mother to tranquillity, if such a thing were possible. Brandy brought a menacing gleam to my mother's eyes. She asked Mirren if she could see the rest of the house, she'd love to see the view from the second floor. Eddy, however, was eager to leave. He had a column to write for the next day and he had had his fill. He suggested that they leave; he could bring my mother to six o'clock mass if they left just then.

'You say we have to go?! To me? I'm not going. I'm staying. I must see the house for me. I didn't see a real house for such a time. You may go, Edward. You go.'

Edward stayed, afraid of what his wife might do, unattended. He was a fool, but I did not tell him so. He would never understand my mother. And she would never understand him. For she was a fugitive refugee, and he was not. The more he might try to chase her, the further into hiding she would go. Eddy would never be able to understand that she did not leave her home by choice. Therefore he could not understand the nature of her madness. We did not leave our house, Eddy, with suitcases neatly packed and a smiling midday sun to set us on the path. We did not wave goodbye with regretful smiles. There was no time for that. Ireland did not seem like a 'nice place to go'. We left in the dead of night with the Russians at our heels. We did not know where on earth we were going. We did not even know if we were going to live. But I couldn't tell Eddy that. My mad mother had sworn me in.

There I was with my third father. I could not tell which was more unreal: the men in mouldy overcoats crouched over the bar in the drab comfort of a midday Dublin pub, or the reeking pungent memories of war. My mother's behaviour did seem strange to Eddy. He had not come across a woman like her before. Could there be something wrong with her?

Comparable to my war years, nothing seems very odd or queer to me. In post-Emergency Ireland it was sex that shocked these people, not war.

The Step was good to me in those days. He too was instrumental in evacuating the Pole in me. He took me from the periphery of the city, where I had trembled upon my graceless, foreign limbs, to the hub of scruffy, bohemian Dublin. He led his crippled protégé to McDaid's and then deeper down toward hell to the Catacombs, where the grouches of literary Dublin lay their heads at night. He asked me, on that gusty afternoon in the Pearl Bar, for the truth about my mother. I had my hands cupped around my empty pint glass. I gazed at the foam in the bottom of it. Eddy was stroking the shredded triangle of hair on his chin. We were ready for another pint. The story of my mother in the ochre house sat between us: a cruel, stentorian clue to my finely concealed past. As Eddy came closer to the question, I began to tap my pint glass. 'Henry, I—'

Confound it! He had begun the sentence with my name: a feat for a man beset by doubt. It was going to be serious. But, if my memory has not been contaminated by the tourist industry, what happened next was that one of the bowsies in the corner dropped his head back, closed his eyes and opened his jaws to the public. Sweet, inebriated song came forth—it might have been Behan. But I was not saved. Edward persisted in his historic quest.

'Henry, what the hell happened out there?'

'Where?'

'In the war.'

'You're the journalist, you tell me.'

'I pretend to know.'

'I see.'

'Do you not remember, is that it?'

'That's it.'

'But she does?'

'Maybe.'

'Was it awful?'

'Time of my life.'

'Come on.'

'I love the Russians and the Russians love me. Same goes for the Germans.'

'She has another son back there.'

'The brother.'

'Was he in the house too?'

'No.'

'Did they make you work hard?'

'Like dogs.'

'Did they feed you?'

'Like dogs.'

'But Ireland seemed a better option, in the end?'

'First choice on the travel brochure.'

'Were there Germans in the house? I mean, how is it she has German?'

'Good education in pre-war Poland.'

'Will you never tell?'

'No point.'

And the songster in the corner bellowed out his chorus.

9

My mother hated Annemarie. My bundly snub-nosed *schatz* Annemarie. She knew nothing of her but her nationality. My mad, hermetic mother believed a German devil had me smitten. No praise for my triumphant final results in college. No praise for my mastery of the German tongue, my extraordinary talents in translation, my diplomatic skills that eased the flow of trade between this shabby backward island and that giant post-war state of industry and competency.

Translating became my sustenance, for a spell. The air grew stuffy in the boardrooms where we met. The Germans on one side, the Irish on the other, a little poorer, a little scruffier, but full of hope. I would sit at the head of the table and through me they would speak. It was I who had the Germans and the Irish laugh in unison, when Nixdorf came to grow computers on our land. The German director, who looked curiously Hispanic to me, told some very *schadenfreude* joke that was bound to force an awkward, sympathetic laugh out of the Irish. I made up another joke and great hoots of laughter erupted on both sides of the desk in unison: the Irish laughing at an Irish joke, the Germans laughing to appreciate the Irish laughter. A tear lodged in the corner of Herr Direktor's eye. It was a happy moment. There were not many. I was fired from the German Translation Services for something akin to slovenliness. They had been respectful of my skill: my fluency was polished to a shine, thanks to Annemarie. But they had been suspicious of this voluminous one-legged Irishman from the very start.

Annemarie was a creature with delicate bones, and fine, mid-brown hair. She had green eyes with a fleck of brown in the left iris. She had long slim fingers that could race across pianos. She had a middle-pitched voice with a husky edge that made her sound like she had not cleared her throat. She could say more, do more, be more than she was. There was always that feeling. She was brimming with potential and garrisoned by pride. But under that pride lay a solid belt of shame. Shame, utter shame, of her nationality.

Nobody else in the department had suspected her of shame, or guilt, or any of the human attributes. She gave a stern impression to both staff and students. But I saw through the veneer. There was nothing harsh or guttural about her: that was a language that had been assigned to her. Good Lord, I never saw a being more moved by music. She had a heart as soft and malleable as a lump of window putty.

I was doing a doctorate on Brecht to pass the time, to defer departure from the bosom of my Alma Mater for as long as I possibly could. I had been in Trinity for eight years. It was upon those very cobblestones that I stumbled across Annemarie Hanke, rushing to a tutorial, late as one of her nationality should never be, sweet and green as the fruit of the greengage tree under which I later arranged to meet her. To talk about Brecht and the brazen *Mother Courage*. I was to discover that Annemarie had never read it. She was, like a terrified schoolgirl, in need of a friend. And Henry had plenty of friendship to give her, plenty of time to relish those slim, stockinged calves that she had brought with her.

Annemarie had fled her father, not her country. Annemarie, my little strudel. I loved those rosy cheeks and that honey-coloured skin. I didn't care where she was from. And yet some untamed part of me did care. Enormously. I felt that through this sallow, acquiescent Teutonic angel, I could redeem myself. I could atone for my dealings with Hilbig, and never disclose them to her. But I fear that my intention was not so lofty—could it have been for the sake of plain old masochism that I sought to have her in my life? That downy peachy face, that was not for masochism. But what was behind that face: I should never have let myself see that.

I was driven by the curiosity to know what she had left behind. Silly old Faustian me. She told me nothing under the greengage tree. I knew then I would have to have her. Gin and orange had a marvellous effect on her. She shed things willingly from her past, and swiftly I gathered them in as they were deposited onto my lap. She giggled and flashed her teeth at me like the girl who had me deflowered and left me for the boat with her one and sixpence ticket. I felt, with Annemarie, more than with any other woman in my life, that I was in the process of acquisition. She would be in my possession for quite some time. And with her I told no lies: though I told no truths either.

Annemarie knew little about the masters of her country. I had to bring her under Goethe's armpit and into Schiller's ears: she hated them as she hated the Fatherland. It was through her father that she learned to hate her country. So it was a great disappointment to her to learn that the only thing the Irish required of her was the propagation of her native tongue. She was employed as a tutor in Trinity's department of German.

One night I brought her to McDaid's and tried to train her tastebuds to the Pint of Plain. The head left a crescent of white foam on her upper lip. She winced. It was like muck, she said. I told her that story about McDaid's having been a meetinghouse for a resurrection sect who had a liking for high ceilings: they provided ample space for apocalypses. She swallowed it whole. It was not a lie. It was lore. Oh, where do I draw the line?

She liked the codgers in the snug who sang the afternoons away. She bought their pamphlets of poetry, read them in my company and forced me into discussions on their style, their content, their influences … she could be such a pedantic bore. I hated when the earnest German in her steamrolled over her coquettish sense of humour. I blamed her father. He had cooped her up in a wooden Bauhaus box dreamed up by Gropius. It was, in its conception, to be an Expressionist variant on the theme of the peasant loghouse. A house full of elbows and white walls. But *der Specht*, the woodpecker, descended on its beams and pecked mercilessly (many more joined him), as if to punish the dwellers within. That was how it all began, she said, with *der Specht*. It was when the birds had begun to peck the attic that Annemarie found her father's papers.

With what he knew, she said, he could have got the chop in Nuremberg. She was repulsed. She was his daughter.

And so it was with Hilbig, for me. Marvellous! Through her I could vicariously dissect my own moral decrepitude. I did not have Hilbig's blood but I shed blood for him when he took away my toe. By subtracting from my physical being he had grafted himself onto me for the rest of my life. Though I had been his victim, he had infected me with his guilt. It is as if, if you come too close to men that mad and fallen, they will not let you leave without rubbing their affliction into your wounds.

Annemarie's father was an architect and had been a committed National Socialist when it suited him, but deserted just in time. He had been on a committee of architects led by Albert Speer who were ordained the task of transforming Berlin into the grotesquely nationalistic city of *Germania* that was the Führer's dream. During the war he was appointed to the Ministry for Armaments. She found his hand-written reports on an underground artillery production camp built in the caves of the Harz Mountains. From its conception in August 1943, it had devoured droves of labour for its purpose. The slaves toiled eighteen hours a day and slept by night in tunnels they themselves had dug. There were photographs of her father in the camp. One showed him beaming with pride beside the Chief Administrator. She did not doubt he knew how the workers had been treated. Granted, he had probably not got wind of the demonic pyres in the East. But for Annemarie this was enough, this slave pit in Thuringia.

It was enough for her that he had smiled as men were decomposing as they worked, rotting in tunnels that led to death. She had nightmares. Men begged for food with their palms held out to her and their eyes wide in their sunken faces. They crawled out of cavernous tunnels on their knees, insane for water and for light. They wheezed like bellows. Ammonia dust had burnt their lungs. They begged Annemarie to ask her father for some food. Every time she woke it was too late. Twenty years too late. She dared not ask her father. From him she hid her eyes until the day she told him she was leaving and she walked out through the garden, plucked one of his prize roses, and left the woodpeckers to peck his Bauhaus down.

Parts of me began to rattle; I thought I'd fall apart. All I could think was, *If she found out, if she found out, if she found out,* beating inside me, faster than my heart. My throat ached to tell her, but I told none of it. I didn't want to upset her, you see. I thought of leaving her to stop myself from giving away too much. But I was thoroughly entwined. God, if only I had left, then.

I held her hand in Dublin snugs and watched tears splash down her cheeks, wishing they were my own. Soon she forgot about her father and the woodpeckers and all the slaves. She fell in love with Dublin and she fell in love with me. I returned her love enthusiastically. We took trips to Connemara. We walked for miles, laughing at the matted sheep, guzzling whiskey, caressing by turf fires. We had never been so free. We decided we should marry.

Late one May we took a posse of Dubliners to celebrate our engagement with a feast. I knew of a pair of Germans in Glenmallin, Co. Wicklow, who ran a reputable inn outside the town. To my surprise, Annemarie did not object to the prospect of a

German feast. Everything had melted into our boon love. I was feeling gallant. So was the Step. He gave us a tidy sum of congratulatory money and lent me his car. Annemarie was very fond of him. She liked his slow, thoughtful conversation and the spark that lit his eyes when he understood you and said 'Ahh'. Annemarie, who was always explaining herself and other things, found this reassuring. She inquired about my mother, but I deflected further interest.

I had the Fischers, the proprietors of this Wicklow establishment, make a banquet of their fare. What a glorious night it was. The tavern, which leans over the side of a hill, gave out an ambered glow through the window at night. Gerry Tallon of the Apollo Gallery was there with Maureen Lindsay, an old flame of mine, clinging to his arm. She was wrapped in a low-cut silver cocktail dress that looked flammable. She had been sulking since the announcement of the engagement, had set about acquiring all sorts of men.

Bernard Byrne waddled along to taste the food. He pressed his inflated belly against the table, and he had some trouble breathing in this position. There were other poets and dramatists. Ranting, raving lunatics who seemed about as literary as a crowd of bachelor farmers. It was their showmanship that sold their books: not the words inside. They pounded their fists and barked at each other across the table.

Michael Grange was late. He slithered in through a crack in the door with a generous spray of flowers. He gave them to Annemarie, who blushed as they fell on her lap. Then, under the candelabra, we began to eat as the agile fingers of our pianist played Liszt upon the *Flügel*.

We started with Beluga caviar and new potatoes, moved on to

French goose liver with truffles on oriental white bread. Mr Fischer's son brought in venison on a long, wide silver tray: a succulent Siberian roast. We had Westphalian ham, black bread and country butter. We had the best German wine the Fischers could get their hands on: Winkler Massenpflug 1957. It slithered down our throats like velvet. We passed on to oriental coffee with mocha chocolate and pralines, gazing drunkenly at the bulbous fruits the Fischers laid out in baskets on the table. A couple of the poets had fallen asleep at the far end of the table. Annemarie and I bid the sleepy banqueters goodnight and went to our room upstairs.

Eddy had joined us briefly, if only to taste a morsel of the venison. My mother was sick, he said. He had to return. I knew what that meant. It had taken every drop of the Winkler Massenpflug to shut her out of my mind. *The extravagance of it. And her. That German girl. How could you?* I had not wished to wake her ghosts. And then, as if she had put a curse on the engaged couple, things began to go horribly wrong. I cringe when I remember what came next. Things were going to be so good! I was going to finish my PhD in Köln, we were going to leave Dublin together and marry in some hulking German Gothic church.

It was late one Thursday afternoon. I had arranged to meet Annemarie in Davy Byrne's at five o'clock after her tutorials. I waited for an hour. I sauntered over to Trinity and found the department empty. Remember: nothing worried me. I was in a cloudless state of mind. It was all honey and flowers and strudel to me. The future glowed. We were to book our tickets to Köln that week. So I went back to Davy Byrne's, only mildly ruffled by Annemarie's unexpected absence. After a couple of pints with Pat Tully I headed home to our flat.

She was in the kitchen, scraping burnstains off an old pot. She did not look up when I came in, but attacked the stains with furious efficiency. Her white knuckles, and her frown. *My little cat.* I came closer to the table, and she got up. She sank the pot into a basin of hot water, and continued to scrape the blackened pot.

'Annemarie?'

'You've been drinking.' She spoke into the black pot.

'Waiting, strudel, for you.'

She swung around to face me. Suds dripped off her hands onto the floor. Usually she would wipe them with a towel. She blew a wisp of hair out of her eye. I wanted to hold her, to feel her crush in me. I could not bear it that I couldn't: something was wrong. She reached into the pocket of her apron. (I had not known she kept things there.) A fly bungled in and out of my ear, and droned away again, toward Annemarie. She handed me the paper. There, trembling in her hand, was my Ahnentafel.

Why, just then, did that cursed document show up? Why had I kept it all those years? I had wanted a memento of my horror, I suppose. But there it was. I was outraged. Blood rushed to my head. My ears stung. My eyes began to water. *You little bitch*, I said. *You prying little bitch.* I snatched the papers out of her hand. I spat and foamed and pounded the walls with my fists. She watched me from the bed. Her hands did not move from her knees. *If only you had told me*, she said.

If I'd told you, you would not have loved me. You would have thrown yourself into the arms of a real, thoroughbred Paddy, one of those poets who knew nothing about what we knew, who had no filthy secrets. And there it was. Hilbig's Ahnentafel that traced my ancestry back to patrician merchants of the Hanseatic League. She thought I was a kraut. A grim reminder of her blighted father. I had lost her. And yet she didn't know the worst of it.

10

We didn't speak for hours, but lay in the half dark on the bed, holding nothing but hands. I wanted to take the confounded document away and burn it, but she still had it in her handbag, and she clutched her handbag strap as tightly as women do in railway stations. As tightly as she clutched my hand. Clutching the two Henrys, at once. Something sloshed about behind my eyes, like heavy treacle. I ached. I never wanted to move or speak again but if I did not I would lose her. I spoke when the streetlights came on.

'We should talk, Annemarie.' But she didn't want to talk. There we were, at a junction in our lives. Afraid to move, afraid to speak, afraid to make it real.

'I thought—I thought you were a Polish refugee.' She said it to the ceiling. Then she took her hand back, and lay it over her belly, like a fish.

'I am, I was, a Polish refugee.'

'Don't lie. Don't be illogical. I have the papers in my bag.' The streetlights flickered outside, and my stomach rumbled.

'Maybe we could have a bite to eat before we talk?'

'No. Tell me who you are.'

'You know who I am.'

'I know who I thought you were.'

'Who did you think I was?'

'Henry Foley.'

'Then that is who I am.'

'Liar! You are Heinrich Malinski! You are a Hamburg aristocrat! Why did you hide it from me?'

'Because it isn't true, my strudel.'

'I have the papers!'

'If you believe them, then I also have a Polish grandmother. And they settled in Lvov.'

'It doesn't matter, it's that you lied!' she shouted, and the lights flickered on the street.

'I never lied.' I said, as quietly as I could. I sat up on the bed and swung my legs over the side, and dropped my head into my hands. The head that held my stories, my life. I was afraid that if I told her, if I started to tell her, that I would never stop, that it would all spill out and then it would be too late. She could do anything with me then, anything.

'Henry, just tell me. Then it will be over.'

'Over? You mean this is the end? We haven't even married. What about Köln? Is that all off? Annie? Annemarie? Oh God, I'm starving.'

'Just tell me, Henry. Then we can talk it over.'

I told her what I could tell her. I told her about Mama going to pick up her hats from the manor on a sunny day in Lvov, about how we were captured by the Oberscharführer and his men. I told her that the Oberscharführer made the Ahnentafel to save us, because my mother was a whore. God forgive me, I said that to save my own skin. I told her that if we had not become Volks-deutsche, we would have died, so I had to thank my mother for that. And I would not be here now with you, if not for that.

'Who was the Oberscharführer, Henry?'

'I can't remember. Please, no more questions. I've told you everything I can remember.' I lay my hand on her knee, but she threw it off.

'Don't lie, Henry. No more lies. Now tell me what was his name.' She'd been studying the Nuremberg Trials, I suppose, she wanted to see if she could match him up.

'Really, I can't—'

'Tell me!' she shouted again.

'No!' I shouted back at her, sick of her at last, she who had made this mess, she had poked her way in ...

'Tell me,' she said slowly, 'or I will really get the next plane back to Köln.'

'You don't know what you're doing, Annemarie. You're killing me. Let's leave it alone.'

'Tell me, Henry. Or else this is it.'

'Hans.' I said. My tongue went dry and my forehead felt hot and damp.

'Hans what?'

'Hans, Hans-I-don't-know.'

'Henry, tell me.'

'All right then! Hilbig! Hilbig! Hilbig! Hans bloody Hilbig!'

I curled up into my pillow and wept into the feathers. There, his name was out. Now, now see what you've done, I said. The name felt plump and greedy in my mouth. I tried to swallow it back down, but it got stuck. The aftertaste was foul. Hilbig, out of my throat, at last. I dribbled on into my pillow, until at last I felt her soft hand stroke my head. I'm sorry, I said. And she said nothing. What was I apologizing for? I hadn't lied, I hadn't lied. I just hadn't told.

In the weeks that followed we were quiet. She did not clatter the crockery in the kitchen. I closed doors with their handles, not my feet. We walked gently on the wooden floors, and in the evenings we sat on rugs together by the fire. To keep the shadows away. But they were there, in corners and the bottom of cupboards. Lurking. I never felt again that I was alone with Annemarie. She sat at tables with her back like a plank, she placed her knife and fork together at the end of meals in the centre of her plate, she sat with her legs crossed, and refused to make love. Daddy, you see, had come back. And it was I, she said, that had invited him. Now she saw her father in poor Henry, in how he made his coffee, and poured it out. In how he flattened the dog-ears out of books, how he shaved from up to down, and how he laughed when he was drunk. Her eyes were always on me, searching for her father in my every move. She wanted to leave me, but she had not found her excuse. Besides, she still wanted to marry me.

Months went by, and then one day I could take no more. It was one morning in September; there were wads of cloud in the sky. I awoke, and turned around to face Annemarie. I stroked her face and her eyelids flickered out of dream. She had slept badly. She had thought to wake me, but decided to wait until the morning. She wanted to ask questions. First thing in the morning. What else happened in the house, Henry? What did the Oberscharführer do to you? What were his responsibilities? What did he look like? Did he flee when the Russians came? Is he still alive? I answered nothing. I got up, got dressed and went about my day. I met Ollie for a pint in McDaid's and found myself in Davy Byrne's for the afternoon with Tully. The sky was as blue as a John Hinde postcard and when I saw Maureen Lindsay walk up Duke Street in a kelly-green mini, I thought: we've got to have a chat.

If Tully hadn't been there, it would have been all right. I could have left Davy's with Maureen, and no one would have bothered. But Tully did. He liked Maureen, you see. Like a fool, I gave Annemarie her excuse.

II

I fell, when Annemarie left. I rolled, blind, into a cold black pit. My mother nursed me. I was neither child nor man. I was a writhing, aching mass of pain. I had thick, black dreams. I heard the thud of soldiers' boots at night marching up the stairs. *Eins-zwei-drei*. I heard tanks a-prowl in the woods. Shadows came out of the corners of the room to steal my voice. I sweated like a pig. I itched, I scratched, I groaned. I saw everything foul and ugly that a man could see.

I took a room in the Stella ward of St Patrick's Hospital. Nobody visited me. Nobody knew where I had gone. There I sat, numb, stale, inert, in my father's paisley dressing gown. My mother came once but I could only stare at her and she left, offended. I ground my teeth and cracked my knuckles and tapped my slipper on the floor. They gave me brightly coloured pills in plastic caps and said Goodmorning Henry how are you today? As if I should reply that all was well, that things had never been better. They had no understanding of what it was like to be a nut. They only wanted us to be better. They wanted their pink, powder blue and yellow pills to bypass pain. I treated my time there as a monastic retreat: I had enforced renunciation, obstinate routine and terrible food. In that sense it wasn't bad. I even made some friends.

I found Laurence Craig, a frail Doctor of English from Trinity, in my ward. As far as I had known he was on sabbatical. I found him on a window seat. His gaze was fixed on an enormous daffodil outside. He had a long beak nose and no chin. Two tiny, pale eyes sat above his nose. At the end of that nose hung a drip, as clear as a drop of spring dew. I wanted to shout boo! so he'd turn in fright and the drip would be flung away. He drew in a breath and shut his eyes, plunged his clawed hand into his pocket and extracted a five-pound note. He sneezed into it, and put it back in his pocket.

'Bless you.'

' 'kyou very buch, 'kyou very buch. Countig by blessigs.'

'Waste of a fiver.'

'Suppose it is.'

'Dead currency in here anyway.'

'That's right, that's right. You been in here long?'

We took a walk outside and examined the daffodil. It was not unusually large. We walked around the garden with our hands in our dressing-gown pockets, in a consensus of silence.

I was afraid. I looked at Professor Craig's skin: flaky, with the dull shine of wax. He had been in for some time. I pulled the string of my dressing-gown tight around my waist and resolved to make a sane man of myself.

'I know what you're thinking.'

Said the professor. I swallowed my excess saliva as quietly as I could.

'What's that, professor?'

'You oughtn't be ashamed of being here, Foley. Talk to Swift about it. He agrees. He built this place so that the harmless would be unharmed by the harmful. We are living in the curls of Jonathan Swift's periwig. We are safe here, Foley. I can assure you of that, if nothing else. Are you listening to me, Foley?'

The poor Professor—he suffered from Menière's Syndrome, as Swift had. How deafening the bells of St Patrick's were to him. He brought me to Lilliput, Laputa, Brobdingnag, Glubbdubdrib

[145]

… forgive me, but the Professor drove me mad. He dragged me around the labyrinth of his inner ears for months, and listened to nothing I said, because he could not hear a word. I was Henry at a loss. The aborted fiancé. The liar. I raged at my sweet, honeyed accuser for not being happy with the way things were. What did it matter if I was known by another name in another place? Why was the past of such importance? Was I then that which I had been? Why did I have to account for it?

I had still not been repaired by the time my stepsister Siobhán came back from London. I had not known that she left because of us. I remembered a thin-lipped flat-bummed girl with pale green eyes and lanky streaked hair who scowled at me in corridors and kicked my wooden leg under the dining table. We were impostors, my mother and I. When Siobhán came back after her stubborn fifteen-year exile, she found her family eroded and worn out. She came to see me in hospital, much to my surprise. I tried to persuade her that in my case things had not always been so bad. I'd had a bad blow. I looked straight into her eyes. She dismissed me with a smile that said, *Oh, Henry, you don't have to do that, you don't have to make excuses.* She looked down at my leg. That was what she remembered best about me: this hinged piece of wood that tried to pass as leg. She remembered a battered Slav with syntactically disastrous English. I could not understand why she was not impressed with what I had become. My flawless accent, my moustache, my education were to her the garnishments of a poor dish. She had predicted this botched evolution. She knew who I was. She could not be fooled. That was why I hated her.

I thought she would ask me questions, but she did not. She was my older, fatter sister entitled to more than I could ever hope for. She had come back to secure her part of the inheritance. And yet she was kind to me. There was a hope in her (and I know this but she never said it) that I would tell her the true story of my childhood. Of who my father was, who my mother was, who the hell my brother was. I know this because I dreamed of it one night after she had visited me. I was in Lvov, in our orchard, with Stanislav. We were shaking the branches of the apple trees to make the petals of the blossom fall, laughing under a midday sun. My parents were standing in a doorway of the house. They turned and went inside. I climbed the tree with Stanislav and we saw, across the fields, beyond the forest, an old plough hauled along by a meaty, piebald horse. He was accompanied by a clown in a German uniform and a dwarf in lederhosen, smoking a pipe. They spotted us in the tree and beckoned us to join them. We gravely shook our heads. Our parents were behind us, looking out the window. The clown took a hamper off the horse's back. He opened it up and pulled out an embroidered cloth and laid it out on the ground. The dwarf put a large jug on the cloth, with four glasses—one red, one blue, one yellow, one green. They laid out chunks of ham, apfel-strudel, chocolate cake, lebkuchen, sausage meats, plums, grapes, oranges and cherries. We jumped from the treetop over the orchard wall and landed in the field. We came and we ate with the clown and the dwarf. Then, in the treetop, I saw Siobhán—plump and full of judgement. I hid under the tablecloth, but it was too late. She had seen everything.

Dreams lean on you in the day. I dream, and sometimes I remember. I experience, and sometimes I remember. Both dream and experience have the potential to become memory. Is there a difference, then, between memory and dream? There are no answers to your questions, Henry. They world stares, ambivalent, at the one who seeks answers. Better to be ambivalent, Henry. Be ambivalent, be numb.

Siobhán gave me a gift of a Philips turntable and a collection of classical vinyl albums. It was these that cured me. These lulled my soul. I crawled out of Swift's periwig, dusted the powder off myself, and waved goodbye to the Professor.

12

I have emerged out of Swift's hospital many times now, unscathed. Every few years, in a black November, I go in. Sometimes I stay until spring. Then I come out and I meet the trembling world, no longer aslant. I can hear what people say. I see the sky, I see the ground, I see the things we have erected between them. It all looks safe and flat again. I stride forth (well, I hobble) and declare myself back from the dead. Where have you been, Henry? I tell them anything they want to hear. Seminars, symposia, conferences, translations—anything they want to hear. Siobhán always kept her promised discretion, as did the Step.

I never did finish my doctorate on Brecht. I tied string around my papers and dug him a snug wee grave. He was buried with my Ahnentafel on a muggy afternoon in May, six weeks after my discharge. Eddy came out to the garden full of concern and curiosity, afraid to approach me but compelled to do so. He stood behind the low garden wall with his hands in his pockets and gave me a half smile.

'What are you doing, Henry?'

There was his fully grown stepson in the garden, hunched up in his raincoat by a pile of earth. Was there any hope for him?

'Preparing.'

'What's in the hole?'

'Preparations.'

I wanted to tell him everything then. To dig up the papers, to throw them at his feet. To unshroud it all. To atone. I could hear a voice in me say Listen, Edward, we want you to know, because you've been so good to us. We want you to know. There was a man called Hilbig, and mummy you know did it with him and I did things too and we told him we hated the Jews and we promised to be good citizens of the Fatherland, all that we did and more, will you still be a husband and a father to us?

It's hardly worth it, is it, coming out with nonsense like that? A long-hidden truth is a precious thing. It should be nurtured and kept safe. I just smiled at my stepfather, and patted the mound that hid my truth. I let him walk away rubbing his thumbs in his clammy pockets. He was puzzled by me. He always had been.

I am proud that I have survived the troughs. I have come to accept their stubborn punctuality.

> How we squander our hours of pain.
> How we gaze beyond them
> Into the bitter duration
> To see if they have an end
> Though they are really
> The seasons of us, our winter –

Rilke. I speak of pain in this quiet room but no one hears me. Thankfully. I speak of pain in my ebb. I whisper into an open fire. If a tear must drop, I let it drop. That proves to me that I have a heart. I resent my foolish friends. It was too easy to trick them into thinking I am this Henry. The Henry they see dancing his limp dance in his great hats and his coloured scarves. Singing, ranting, flattering, cursing, insulting, imbibing. Why did they accept me? Why did Oliver, of all people? Why did he not once in all the years ask me to look into his eyes and tell the truth of who I am? He could have. After our sodden night by the canal when he told me about what the Brothers did to him. Why not then? Why did he not question my evasion? Why did he not call out after me as I dragged my leg down the canal path away from him, away from those ignorant swans that made us look so desperate and so haggard? Why did he let me limp away like a coward? He, of all people.

Those were bad times, after St Pat's. I convalesced in my parents' house. Other worlds were falling apart. Across the hunchback field the Hawkinses were getting old, too old to minister to the needs of their geriatric home. Its wooden beams were rotting, its walls were drenched with damp, the slates were falling from the eaves like autumn leaves. All this insinuated ruin. There were so many things to attend to in the house: the fires, stoves, gardens, sheds, stables, cellars and the warren of rooms that had never been inhabited. They moved to the gate lodge. They had a badly attended auction and sold the house for a pitiable sum. The remnants of the auction have been squatting in my apartment since the day the bidders turned them down. That is how I come to have these scratched Chippendale chairs. That is how I came to have the George II candelabra, the silver sauceboat, the William IV pumpkin-shaped silver teapot, the oriental silver Buddha, the rosewood hunting table and this very fine nineteenth-century gilt mirror, which I am gazing into at this very minute. Mine. Mine, since I have been their warden for such a time. Tristan Hawkins can go to hell. These are my children. I have polished them and varnished them and waxed them for two decades. They are the trophies of my trade. They were the chosen ones. The clumsy Victorian chairs, the clubfooted Chippendale table and other less reputable chattels I sold on Francis Street. So began my haggling days, so ended academe for me.

I got a decent trade going with the capital that came from the Hawkins' furniture and a good deal of borrowed money that was never paid back. I rented a shop on Francis Street. Foley's Curios, No. 37. It was in the antique shop on the opposite side of the street that I found that well travelled little samovar. It delights me to find objects that have strayed so far from home. How many hands have fondled them, how many eyebrows have been raised in speculating over their value? Poor, lost chattels. Unwitting victims of larceny, plundering, ransacking, smuggling, marauding. We are all, we merchants of antiques, receivers of stolen goods.

There were other four-legged teapots. I stole one of them when Dr Hawkins barred me from the house. I found it blackened in their cellar but I knew that it had some value. I have a sense for these things. When Tristan had gone to bed I bolted across the field with it under my furballed duffel coat. That he should have so much when I deserved so much seemed unfair. I took other things: a silver table bell, a spirit flask, napkin rings, a machine-turned nine-carat gold cigarette case that came to the value of six hundred and fifty pounds. I pawned it for a binge. Silly Henry.

The Hawkinses never noticed. These heirlooms they perceived en masse. Detail escaped them. I took every advantage of that. It's fair compensation for what I lost. What do I have of my country manor home but a few botched memories and a long way home? What do I have? What did my mother have? What does Stanislav have?

It came so suddenly, this decision to return. My mother died three months ago. I spent my life gnawing through our bond, trying to break it. But only death could do that. On my way to her sickbed I passed through her garden. There was nothing left of it. No nasturtiums, no irises, no Lvov sunflowers. There were a few wild strawberries and a crowd of filthy dandelions, delighted to have their way in the garden again. Stray bricks lay on the grass. Her preened, combed garden pre-empted her death. The curtains in her room were drawn. Her bedside lamp was on: a dull light hovered in the corner of the room. There was a droning sound, perhaps it was her wheeze. It had been a decade since I'd seen her room. A small, framed image of Our Lady hung above her head. An embroidered card with the rosary in Polish was stuck to the wooden frame with a brass thumbtack. There was the smell of age in the room: talcum powder, old medicine, stale, unmoving air.

When I saw her I was seized by the thought that what was nestling in her lungs was the smoke from Hilbig's evening fires, the dirt of all those years. I had seen her as ill as this in one of the war's winters. I had seen her lying under a bearskin in the upstairs room with lather on her forehead and poor, bruised eyes. Ice had cracked on the windowpanes. You could not see outside. My mother prayed she would outlive the war.

Now this faded thing was before me again, with her lank hair hidden behind her neck and those shadows resettled around her puckering eyes. Worn to a shadow, she was. Poor Mumsy. Each day I came back, some more of her had been chiselled away. Dr

Hawkins said she needed to be hospitalized but she would not go. My mother beckoned me to her bedside and whispered to me: 'Whatever happen, bury me under brzoza.'

Eddy bounded over from the invigilator's chair. The silver birch, do you mean, Elizabeth? Would you like to see them? He was hoping to God he could rip the curtains open and let some daylight in. She did not understand him. He was so proud to have remembered the word *brzoza*. The only thing he understood about her. The rest was a puzzle: the stubborn reclusion, the neurotic frugality, the bone under her pillow, the thick Slavic tones undaunted by forty-five years in the Wicklow hills. To her he had been nothing but a husband. A man whose roof she could crouch under, whose floors and walls she could perform ablutions upon. She was horrified by the mould that would sneak across the walls in winter and contaminate the food. She never accepted that things were, by nature, damp and squelchy here. She longed for dryer, terser air. For the crunch of snow. For a more soldierly man than Edward. He was too clement. But Edward was so curious about her. He studied her in her sleep, stalked around her like a hungry dog, and scampered away when she woke.

There he was beside her deathbed, seeking his long-denied ratification. And yet, as she slipped away from him under the folds of Our Lady's dress, he knew his communion with her was not to be. Dr Hawkins announced an embolism. My mother was choking to death. Mirren Hawkins came with flowers and grapes. Age had reduced her to a less daunting height. She had developed a stoop and became, by necessity, a more modest sort of woman. Mirren had scorned those who did not wade through life with wellingtons and pride. My mother had been her mute antithesis.

[153]

Death wheezing away in the house like that; it just wouldn't do. One day before she died, I walked out into the hissing drizzle to the woods below the house. The air was thick and humid. A heavy, numb feeling settled on my brow. A faint ringing sounded in my humidor. I had not been humorous in weeks. I had not even smiled. Henry, unadorned. No rings, no hats, no song, no bellows of laughter. Something was afoot. Henry was missing. What had happened? Mumsy had her grim reaper, at last. She'd been waiting all her post-war life. But it was dawning on me: Henry would be left behind. She was deserting me. I had so wished to desert her. The smell of wild garlic rose in the muffled air. Bluebells had crowded under the trees. A wide stream twisted through the woods, mumbling on its way. The trees seemed huge. They sank into the ground with graceful, tendoned boles. Under the peeling bark a crowd of bugs fled my giant hand. Everything in the forest was alive. Not just Henry, as I had always imagined. How could my mother not have seen? Why was she leaving this behind?

It might have been the moment I thought that, that she died. I had rambled into the thick of the woods. I had not heard Father Lacey's car engine pelting up the rocky drive. I knew, as soon as my foot was in the house, that she was dead. There was a numb hush. In the room, they did not look up. Father Lacey put his broad hand on my shoulder, and squeezed it. My mother looked young and waxen. My stepfather leaned over and whispered, 'She said to say goodbye. To you and Stanislav.' And Stanislav.

That night, when they peeled away the bedclothes they found her fist clenched around that curious little bone. I put it in the coffin with her. Bye bye, Mama. As my mother had possessed nothing, she left nothing of significance behind her. Except two sons.

Stanislav and I. The dregs of war. I did not expect to feel like this. Logically, her death should have been the solution to my problem. She should have taken her memories to the grave with her. But her death has made memory the more redolent, as if her memories had been grafted onto mine. Henry's gone all melancholy. Not like him at all. But Mumsy's gone. I have never felt more alone. All's aslant again. All is muffled. When I close my eyes indignant pictures of the past rise to greet me after their long burial. I have seen Stanislav again: a young boy with bruised knees in grey shorts smiling by the door of a peasant's house. A large man with a sack on his back is stacking up a farm cart. I can smell earth and an open fire and bread baking in an oven. The door of the house shuts closed. It is dark. Which side am I on?

13

Since her death, I have been raw. I have been trying to pack, for Poland. The world of Henry Foley is a cluttered one indeed. His tea-gown, his kimono, his dressing gown, his smoking jacket, his mufti, his tatters, his old rags. His hats—the caps, the berets, the tam o' shanter, the boater, the bowler, the sombrero. His shoes—the boots, slippers, sandals, goloshes, spats. His gloves—goatskin, sheepskin, mittens, muffs. His jewels—brooches, tie pins, cufflinks, watches, pocket watches, chains, rings gold and silver with a kaleidoscope of gems. There are warehouses full of his chattels. The things he cannot sell in Sunday markets. Furniture, paintings, crockery, cutlery, glass, rugs, carpets. Gods, divest me. Disinherit me, punish me.

It happened, you see, when I went back to the Step's house after the funeral. In the kitchen, I saw my mother in the little things she left behind. She had saved used matches, poured excess oil into jars, wrapped old food in foil. I saw the genius of her resourcefulness. How she had saved things, in case. The seeds from her garden were kept in matchboxes in the larder: hundreds of them were meticulously packed, labelled and stacked together. From these little boxes another garden could hatch. Paradise could be regained. And in the cupboards, stuck to floral contact paper, were her pickles. Onions and gherkins, trapped in jars.

I found letters from my brother Stanislav, I found letters to him written in her timid schoolgirl's hand. One of them was dated 12 December 1946. The year we had come to Ireland. She couldn't send it because the authorities would have eaten it up. She was very sad, she said. She wished that Stanislav could come to Ireland. He was every day in her heart and her thoughts. How was Aunt Magdalena? Was the winter cold? Was he eating well? I set the letter down on my lap. I could not read the rest because I could not understand the Polish, because my eyes were wet with tears. Had I forgotten all of this? My mother had a son. I had a brother. Once we had had a father and we all lived together in a house in the east of Poland.

Eddy found me in my mother's room, rummaging through piles of paper. Our Lady watched us from over the bed with that manufactured-looking melancholy dripping from her face. My mother's inept deputy.

'Are you all right, Henry?'

'No.'

'You're upset, I see.'

'You're observant.'

'Are you all right?'

'I'm going back.'

'Where?'

'To Poland.'

My brother Stanislav. Fellow tenant of my mother's womb, fellow evictee. My orchard companion. My grey-shorted, scabby-kneed brother by the open farm cart, by the closed door of the peasant's home, by the smell of baking bread and earth. That is all I can remember.

'Come on,' said my mother, 'we have no time.'

With no time, we left. Did I wave to Stanislav? Or was he already shut behind that giant door? Why did he not jump onto the farm cart with us? Why did he not come home with us? Why did he not fall under Hilbig's hand? It is dawning on me slowly that I do not know much. Oh, Henry. What have you done? You have bought a ticket to see a man you hardly know.

I went to the Polish Embassy and charmed a blonde secretary into translating Stanislav's letter. She had a beautiful, flawed smile: her right eyetooth had a dark brown stain. She was slim but her ankles were thick as if some excess bottom flab had wriggled down her hips and settled down there. She said I said 'dzien dobry' with an impeccable accent. I tried to cajole her into giving me a quick lesson but she refused, saying she had 'tayribul lot of work to do, sir.' There was a book beside her telephone. The cover showed a handsome, airbrushed couple gazing into each other's metallic eyes. An emery board marked a page in the middle of the book. She would continue reading it after I had left. When she paused to file her nails she would wonder, absently, who that crippled man with the hat had been, the one who had left a generous ten-pound note for services rendered, the one who had said goodbye and thank you in perfect Polish, but claimed he hadn't got a word.

It wouldn't do to find yourself fumbling for a common word with a brother that you hadn't seen in fifty years, grimacing like a pair of dumbstruck fools. I shall pray in Polish that there be some fluency between us. I kept my mother's prayer card for such emergencies. Drink will come to aid, I'm sure. It does wonders for jolting a clogged-up memory. I have been known, in inebriated states, to speak languages that have long lain dormant in my mind, that had not crossed my tongue since early in my schooldays. I remember standing beneath a Gothic window in McDaid's, invoking my neglected Lord with a rendition of his Prayer in Latin. Annemarie was impressed. It was the gin. Gin always makes a pious man of me. There were other times my tongue was loosened by the sharp sting of alcohol. Once I spoke with a Greek tourist in some strange dialect of his ancient tongue. We were drinking ouzo by a bush in Stephen's Green, with the mallards waddling about at the edge of the pond and the swans being all disdainful as is their wont. Mitrakos told me he made amphorae for the tourist stalls in Athens. He had a little factory in Crete. I still have the amphora that he gave me: Eros is displayed in red figure, doing wicked things to nymphs. At least, that is my interpretation of it.

In my stupor I poured ouzo into Eros' amphora and we downed it like proper little Bacchanalians. My Grecian friend collapsed and I sang myself to sleep. When I woke up I found I was still clutching the amphora. The empty bottle lay exhausted on its side. Mitrakos had vanished like a sylph. The madness of the islander: that is a thing to consider.

Enough of my stories. I was speaking of language. I remembered my Greek and Latin. But there is no liquid that could dislodge my childhood Polish. Hilbig put a stiff clamp on that. It is the language of the orchard, of baking bread, of a field of sun-flowers and a flying stork, of silver birches, of the Schveetheart tailors, of a dead father and a lost brother. After fifty years I will taste the Polish tongue again. It will bring me back across the gully to my forgotten side. What of all that lay between? Will he want to speak of that? What will he know of Hilbig? Oh God. I will be Henryk again. I am not ready. But I am compelled.

They still don't understand, these people. Even Ollie. He keeps disappointing me. Yesterday in Neary's he asked me did I think I'd be safe out there, did I think I'd be able to get back? He has some irrational, superstitious fear about the Eastern Bloc. Communism has fallen, I told him. Walesa and John Paul brought them on a holy, solid road to freedom. Democracy, Ollie. Poor Ollie. He is afraid I'll get my backside pinned between a Soviet tank and a towering cement block with some foaming Russian holding a Kalashnikov to my head. Maureen is so afraid I'll disappear she suggested, or demanded, that she accompany me to Poland. She wouldn't say a word while I was with my brother. She'd go off shopping. One doesn't go, I told her, to newly born post-communist countries to go shopping. She took offence. She took my rebuff as new evidence of my secret Slavic lover. And so I go to Poland without Maureen's blessings. And now that my departure is imminent, and I am anxious to my bones, I feel I wouldn't mind her company. Her constant yabber and accusation would be a comfort.

I collected my ticket yesterday. I am to be in Dublin airport at 8 a.m. for check-in on the fifteenth of September. I fly Dublin–Heathrow–Frankfurt am Main–Breslau–Warsaw. After three air-borne hours and four hours of waiting in airport lounges, my feet will be on Polish land. Maureen dropped in to say goodbye this evening. When she saw the ticket, she snatched it off the table. She came back into the sitting room and draped her shawl over the back of my chair. Her hand trailed across it as she moved toward the fire. I offered her a drink. She smiled at me: Our Lady of the Gin and Tonics. God knows why she bothers with this ritual of coquetry. She handed me back my ticket, batting her clotted eyelashes at me, and bolted down her drink. The crapulent hag. Then she asked me for another, and her promenade began. She always did this in my home. She would saunter up and down the room, glancing proprietorially at everything I owned. She had a foolish fancy that it would all be hers one day, just because she'd been the cause of Annemarie's deserting me. She didn't know that I still expected my strudel back one day. I had even written to the Bauhaus in Köln to say I'd be stopping by in Frankfurt, if she had any time. I got no word back, of course.

This evening Maureen wanted to make a last stab. She reached for her bejewelled evening bag and took out a cigarette. She lit it and blew smoke at me.

'Henry, what's all this about?'

That prying, stifling Dublin familiarity: it was beginning to choke me. Their curiosity is grotesque; it is dangerous here to have a secret. They can smell them. How many times have I been lured into a public house and asked, sweetly, to cough up? And when you don't they cast at you a hurt leer and the bitter insinuation that they will damn well find out anyway.

'What's all what about?' I asked, and offered her a chocolate. She took a praline to please me.

'You know fine well, Henry. You know fine well.'

A fine net of smoke settled in her hair. I walked to the other side of the room and poured myself a whiskey. She was rooted to the chair. She would not leave until she had what she wanted tucked safely between her withered, sagging breasts. She wanted a neat, well-sown story about a Slav that I loved, that I bedded, that I impregnated. As long as it all ended in misery she would be happy. I had no such story, but I could have spun it and she would have believed it because she liked Henry the Charlatan. She laughed at his vulgar jokes, sang along with his songs, feigned love when he feigned love, clapped for him, egged him on, fawned over him.

'Come on Henry, who is she?'

She stubbed out her cigarette. It lay there mutilated, with its black butt facing me. There was a glob of lipstick on the filter. She lit another.

'Maureen, there is no woman.'

'So why are you going?'

'I told you.'

'Rubbish. Long lost brother my arse. For God's sake just tell me what you're up to.'

'I'm going to Poland to see my brother.'

'You're not going there for good are you, Henry? You wouldn't leave little Maureen here on her own would you? This brother isn't gay, is he Henry? Is that what this is all about?'

'Maureen, it's very simple. You are Irish, and I am Polish. That is the difference between us.'

'You were only born there. You were bred here.'

'I shed blood for my country, Maureen.'

'You are mad, Henry. You were only three or something.'

'I shed blood.'

'How?'

'A Nazi cut off my toe. An SS man. He imprisoned me and my mother in our own home for three years ...'

'That's the best yet!'

She cackled into her empty glass, lost in her triumphant laugh. This was the best yet: the truth. The truth was just another tall, wide, impossible story. I asked her how she thought I had come to lose the lower half of my left limb. Gout, she said, you dirty old blaggard. She will never believe me, thank God. My secrets are safe.

Ollie is driving me to Dublin airport at six forty-five in the morning: to be safe. Ungodly! I feel ill. The phone rang today and I am sure it was my brother, or some representative of his. A Polish operator, if there be such a thing. They asked in the same muggy, defiled English as my mother's, if I was here. Ees Henry? I said hold on, hold on I'll get him. For in that moment I had left myself and indeed I was not there. By the time I had collected myself the voice had gone, and left behind it an eerie engaged tone.

Oh, My Lord! Henry is off for a holiday! I'd better pack. Toothbrush. Shaver. Razors. Pyjamas. Spare bolts for the leg. Clean socks. Clean underpants. Hair wax. My new silk tie. My green cravat. Marmite. Kerrygold. Hipflask. Longjohns. Thermals. Perfume for his wife. Sweets for his children. Records. Books. Aftershave. My valise. My tweeds. Which hat? My medicines. I must not forget a thing. I have no time. But I'll be back. I'll be back with a valise full of stories.

3

Stanislav and Henry

I

It was a warm evening. An indolent bird flew east. Outside Kraków Central Station, a taxi driver was quarrelling with a woman over her fare. She had three large cases lined up beside her like children. She covered her face in her hands and began quietly to weep. Everybody saw her. The pretzel vendors, the flower vendors, the fruit vendors, the man in the fast-food kiosk. They all saw. Passers-by snatched glances at her. The other taxi drivers, who had been sleeping or smoking in their rank, leaned out of their car windows and watched drowsily. They knew Marek. He never bartered. He never used his meter. He was a mule. Too bad for the lady. She should have asked the price before she got in.

The taxi driver revved his engine and drove to the front of the rank. Dust rose up from under the tyres and sprinkled itself over the lady. She coughed and rubbed her eyes. She scowled at the departed taxi. Everybody was still watching her.

A few minutes later another taxi drove up. It was a grey Fiat. Its back bumper was hanging loose. A large man in a beige jacket and an open shirt got out. He combed his fingers through a swab of thick black hair that had fallen over his eye, and patted his forehead with a damp handkerchief. He held a piece of cardboard in his left hand. With his right hand he pressed a note into his driver's fist, took the change, thanked him, bade him good evening, turned toward the station doors, and stopped. There was a beautiful woman in a blue print dress trying to haul two suit-cases along the ground, and kicking a third in front of her. He caught up with her and asked if she needed help. She smiled, and brushed her hair behind her ear. He stuck his piece of cardboard under his armpit and made a swoop toward the two heaviest pieces. They walked together to her platform. Her train to Katowice was to leave at ten to seven, and she had a connecting train from there to Prague. She told him all about the taxi driver. He listened intently. A band of perspiration broke out on his forehead. Drips bled down the arch of his large nose. His armpits dampened, and the piece of cardboard slithered down the inside of his arm. He stopped. He asked the lady would she carry it for him, and as she was taking it, he noticed her long and silky eye-lashes. She asked him why he had the piece of cardboard with him. He had to meet someone, he said, whom he didn't know. *A woman*, thought the lady. *A foreigner*, said the man, *whose name is printed on that piece of cardboard. But Malinski is a Polish name*, she said. *Doesn't matter*, said the gentleman, *he's not from here. What is your name, madame?* Her name. Agnieszka Topol-ska. Pleased to meet you, Pani Topolska, I am Jan Pachocki.

It was seven o'clock, time to part. Jan Pachocki was fifteen minutes late to meet the foreigner off the Warsaw train. He kissed his lady's hand. He could still smell his wife's Russian dumplings in the sleeve of his jacket as he wiped the sweat from his upper lip with it. The jacket she had stitched the evening before. He had to go. He made his way to platform five.

The train was sitting at the platform, empty. Everyone had left. Jan winced. Had he missed the foreigner? He confirmed with the stationmaster that it was the express train from Warsaw. There were three other men on the platform. A drunk had his legs sprawled before him on a bench and a bottle of cheap wine in his fist. His hiccups startled him, occasionally, to life. A young man with a moustache was leaning against a pillar. He was fidgeting nervously with the cuffs of his open shirt. The stationmaster kept a furtive eye on him. There was one more: a fair, tall, plump man in a black hat, a tweed jacket and a green felt waistcoat. His coat was draped over his shoulder. He heaved a crippled leg along the platform with the help of a silver-topped cane. The *tap-tap-tap* of the cane echoed in the silent, hollow cavern of Kraków Central Station.

Jan lifted his piece of cardboard up for everyone to see. At once the cripple swivelled on his good leg at the far end of the platform. He looked at Jan, squinted and wrinkled up his nose. He threw his arm up in the air, dropped his newspaper, and shouted across the platform: 'Yooo hooo!'

The drunk woke up and cast a bleary red eye on him. He took a slug of his wine, and a drip bled down his jaw. The young man stepped back behind the pillar as the stranger passed him by.

'Yoo hoo! It's Henry. Stanislav, is that you?'

Jan stuffed the cardboard sign into his jacket pocket, and held out his hand.

'Pleased to meet. I should say, I must say, I am not Stanislav. I am Jan Pachocki.'

'I'm Henry. Henry Foley. That name on the board's a bit old. So—so you're not my brother?'

'No, I am sorry. We will go together to his home. It would not take long. Some twenty minutes, something like that. Stanislav is waiting for you.'

'I see.'

'Pan nie moge mowic po polsku?'

'Sorry? Oh, no. No I don't speak Polish. I've forgotten. Forgotten it all.'

When Henry had seen *Henryk Malinski* scrawled in charcoal on the cardboard sign, he knew his brother was expecting a Pole. After fifty years he was still expecting a Pole.

'You have no baggage?'

'Lost. All lost. Five damn people on a propeller plane from Frankfurt to Warsaw and they damn well lost it. The bloody fools.'

'I am sorry, I beg your pardon?'

'Lost. They lost it. All I've got is my duty-free.'

'Katastrof. All baggage?'

'They said they'll send it down tomorrow. They found it in bloody Beirut or Damascus or some place like that.'

'I am sorry?'

'THEY SAID THEY'LL SEND IT HERE TOMORROW!'

'To station?'

'No. Not to station. To Stanislav.'

'Aaah. Rozumiem. Now I understand. So you have no baggage. We can walk to centre and take tram. Is it OK for you?'

'Sounds lovely. Fine. Could do with a drink.'

'Ah, you are hungry?'

'Drink. Need a drink.'

'So we can drink.'

'Good idea. Bloody good idea.'

'Dobrze. Let's go.'

Under the stained trees in the Planty, Henry wondered would he ever get his suitcase back. He remembered his green cravat, his Viyella shirt and his paisley dressing-gown. In his mind he saw them flapping through the sky in a sort of aerial caravan, flying away from him forever. He sighed. Jan offered him a cigarette. Henry took one of the short, fat filterless cigarettes and thanked him. Jan lit it for him with a match that threw out a loud flame, lighting up his whole face. There was something ritualistic in how Jan extinguished the match with a neat twist of his index finger and his thumb, and flicked it away onto the grass. Jan chuckled, but Henry had no idea why. They puffed, and Henry coughed out a cloud of thick dry smoke. As the smoke dispersed he saw they were coming to a large, open square. It was quiet and dark. There were no streetlights. A few tinny cars had passed them by as they had walked across from the station, but that was all. Everything seemed to be closed. As they walked onto the square, Jan took a long drag of his cigarette, and told Henry, as he exhaled, that Kraków was a great city of culture. He said it gravely, as if he had some secret duty to his city. Henry felt like a bland, ill-informed tourist. He did not feel like he had come to be reunited with his brother after fifty years. And anyway, he thought, why did Stanislav not come to meet me at the station? They stopped under the shadow of a vast Gothic church that was pitched at an angle to the square. Jan pointed to the two spires of the Mariacki Cathedral, which are of unequal height.

'You see those towers?'

'Yes.'

'There is a legend of two brothers who hated each other. One constructed his tower faster than the other. The slower brother killed him with a knife. You are still hungry?'

Henry swallowed the morbid little tale and smiled politely. No, he said, I'm not hungry. Jan chuckled and hurried on, remembering how anxious poor Stanislav would be. He had left Stanislav that afternoon polishing his jars of pickles. He said he had no time, and asked if Jan could collect his brother. Stanislav had made the cardboard sign.

Henry flicked his cigarette away into the mammoth, unlit square, and caught up with Jan. At the end of a short street they came to a feeble shelter and waited for the number six tram. Henry looked back at the tall Italianate buildings that graced the square. Smug: they had survived the war. Henry turned away, faced the shelter and said something inconsequential about the weather. The tram came rattling up the tracks, ringing a shrill bell. Henry felt ill. He clutched his mother's prayer card and smiled at his brother's friend. They embarked.

The lights in the tram flickered as they passed St Francis' church. The drunk who had been on the platform staggered to the front of the tram, where Jan and Henry were sitting. He lunged toward the back of Henry's seat and hauled himself up beside him, as if they were old friends.

'Przepraszam pana, przepraszam pana-czkawka-czy ma pan papierosy?'

Henry looked into his inflamed eyes, smelt the sweet putrid smell of booze and did not understand. Jan gave the drunk a cigarette; he always did. The drunk wiped spittle from the corner of his mouth and staggered back to the other end of the tram. He crouched beside a seat, clutched the bottom of a handrail and settled into conversation with himself. When Henry and Jan were getting out, the drunk shouted 'Kanado, kocham cie!' at Henry, and glared at him.

'What did he say?' Henry asked Jan, when they were out.

'He said, "I love you Canada". I don't know why. He's so drunk he doesn't even know what language we are talking.'

They were standing outside a hulk of a supermarket with a green neon sign lit over its doors. One of the letters was not working and hung lopsided, buzzing like a trapped fly. Henry saw, across the wide river, a floodlit castle. They walked on.

'Wawel Castle,' said Jan. 'The old seat of the Polish kings.'

They walked down onto an unlit street and took a path that led down to the riverbank. Henry saw the swans sleeping. He remembered the Royal Canal in Dublin. No, it was not the same. This was not the safe, trained track of water that circumscribes the city of Dublin. This was a river that would flow robustly into other rivers, in other countries. Only the swans were the same. For the love of God, thought Henry, my leg is killing me. Are we ever going to get there? Are we not having a bloody drink?

At half past eight they came to the door of a 1930s apartment block. Something in the river splashed, and a dog howled down the path. There was a light on in a room on the top floor. A figure came to the window and opened it. He leaned out over the sill and called his friend.

'Jan.'

'Jestesmy. Przyjechal.'

Loud, conspiratorial whispers. Henry clutched the top of his silver-topped cane. That was his brother, up there. A set of keys came hurtling down from the window and fell with a crash like a handful of coins at Henry's foot. Jan opened the door and Henry hobbled in. It was dark but for a few lean bars of moonlight that extended from the windows to the walls. A door opened on the first floor. An old woman with a round, cracked face came out. She wiped her hands on a floral apron.

'Dobry wieczor. Witamy,' she said to Henry.

'She welcomes you,' said Jan.

'Ah, good. Hello. Thank you. *Dziekuje.* Good night. Oh dear.'

The smell of red cabbage and warm milk had followed the old woman. She reeked, to Henry, of familiar things. He held his nose. He did not notice the cracked, broken slats on the wooden stairs and the missing pane in the window with branches poking through. At the top of the building there was a vase with dried flowers on a shelf in the corner of the tiny landing. A bare bulb lit the space. There was a bell set in the frame of the door. Henry smiled, in the dim light, his earnest tourist smile. Jan sank a large brass key in the lower lock and rattled it until it clicked. He opened the top lock with a small flat key. Finally, he took a key with tiny hemispheres carved into it. He turned this in the central lock twelve or thirteen times. He plunged his hand down on the door handle and swung the door open. Henry found himself in another dark hallway. There was a door at the end of it, slightly ajar. There was a crack of light.

Stanislav came out and turned on the light in the long hall. He saw his brother: well fed and well dressed. Henryk, the apple of his dead mother's eye, coveter of the red toy train. Henry saw a man in a slate-blue suit with thinning hair. His skin was stretched sparingly over polished cheekbones. The brothers perched, for a moment, at the edge of the gulf between them and smiled at one another. Henry held out his hand, and limped toward his brother. Stanislav wondered if Henryk had been injured in the war. The brothers shook hands and as they looked into each other's eyes, each saw his mother. They looked away.

'Witaj, Henryk.'

'Thank you, good to see you again—I mean—do you speak English?'

Stanislav looked to Jan, who shrugged, as if to say: You should have considered that a man who has not set foot on Polish soil for half a century would be a little rusty. They filed into the apartment. In the hallway, the timed light switched off just after they had shut the door.

2

When Henry awoke, his throat felt tight and dry. He swallowed, and cast his eyes about the room. He had slept in his brother's room, Stanislav had slept on the couch. There was a plant on the table by Henry's bed, dry as paper. Beside it, there was a photograph of a ballet dancer enclosed in a small, brass frame. Henry wondered if that was the wife. A bookcase took up most of the wall that faced him. He could not read any of the titles. Ah, Poland, he thought. This is Poland. Outside the window, through the white nylon curtains he could see a clear sky and an autumn treetop. He had not expected this. He had forgotten that Poland's meteorological cycle did not consist of two extreme seasons, one of sunflowers and one of snow. He laughed at himself for bringing his thermals, and then remembered that they were lost. He cursed the airline, and thought of his breakfast. What would be in store for him? Would his brother look the same this morning? What were they going to talk about? He lifted his leg out of bed and threw on his stale shirt.

In the kitchen, Stanislav was preparing breakfast. He took some sausage and some sheep's cheese out of the fridge and laid them on the table beside the bread. He went into the sitting room and looked at the rows of jars he had arranged on his drawing board. He folded up the crumpled bedclothes on the couch. He had slept well, thanks to his brother's whiskey. It had been the first time he had tasted Irish whiskey. The sweet, nutty taste scalded the gullet as well as any spirit. Henryk's giant pink fish had not pleased him so much. A strange offering, he had thought. He did not like fish, as a rule. Carp at Christmas was enough. He had only seen the sea once. He didn't like the smell of seaweed, the way the sea heaved itself on and off the land. He didn't like the thought of eating those big-eyed, scaly creatures that men pulled out of it with hooks: surely that was food for another species? He had only eaten Henryk's salty smoked fish to be polite. Henryk, he said to himself, you will taste Poland when you sink your teeth into these Krakovian meats! How had Henryk become so unPolish? Where had his Polish gone? How could Mama have let that happen? Stanislav had not learned English to communicate with the English or the Irish or the Americans. He had learned it because he liked English Gothic architecture. He had not known, when he was combing the neat columns of English architectural periodicals, that he would one day use those words to speak to a brother he had not seen in forty-nine years. Jan had done most of the talking the night before. When he left they went to bed almost immediately, bidding each other goodnight with the cordiality of strangers who just happened to be in the same hotel. The war and Mama sat between them: silent memorials.

Stanislav put the sausage slices on a plate, lit a cigarette, and waited for Henryk to join him. A few minutes later he heard the muffled tap of the cane on the sitting-room floor.

Henry came in. Stanislav moved some plates and cups from the sink to the draining board.

'Good morning, Stanislav. What is it you say? Dzien dobry.'

'Dzien dobry. Won't you please have some breakfast?'

'Breakfast?'

'Sniadanie.'

'Shnadanee.'

'Bardzo dobrze. Very good.'

'Barstodobdee. Sounds like one of Gulliver's islands.'

'You will learn Polish again, I think.'

'Your English is good. Thank God for that, eh?'

'No, tayribul. I never learned in school because of Russians. I learned because of my research. Jan helped me. Please, some breakfast.'

'Thank you.'

'Ah! But first I must show you something very special. Come, please, come.'

He showed Henry a bureau by the window of the sitting room. Very nice, Henry thought. Very nice, a walnut and marquetry bureau with a cartouche-shaped back. Very nice indeed. Worth about three grand? Stanislav opened the hinged front and lowered it carefully over the supports. He pulled open one of the small wooden drawers and took out an old fountain pen and a pince-nez. He attached the pince-nez to his nose and pretended to write with the pen, looked up at Henry and laughed a wheezy laugh that made his eyes water. Henry was baffled. He knew he was supposed to appreciate this histrionic display, but its meaning was lost on him. He hoped that his brother was not mad.

'You don't remember?'

'Remember what?'

'Our father.'

'Not very well.'

'This is his desk. I can—look—still to hear him writing if I—look.'

Stanislav leaned his ear down upon the desk. He sat there, for a half a minute or so, with his eyes fully closed. Henry gripped the top of his cane, stared out the window, and fixed his eye on the farthest point. When Stanislav got up, Henry showed his tourist's smile. Stanislav told Henry to press his ear against the desk.

'Can you hear it, Henryk? Can you hear it?'

'No. I hear nothing.'

'It's the memory. I can hear it. Papa's pen moving.'

'My hearing isn't that good.'

'You do not remember this desk? Papa's desk?'

'No. It's very nice, but I don't remember. How did you get it here from Lvov?'

'Was sent after the Russians came to Magdalena Dobczowska, our aunt. Mother of my sister. I mean, I mean sister of our mother.'

'Aunt Magdalena, I've heard of her.'

'Henryk, you must know, you must know that one time before, you were in this apartment. Przed wojna. Before war. We came from Lvov together to a—pogrzeb—? You know, when a person dies there is a special ceremony—'

'A funeral.'

'Exactly. Funeral. And one time for Wszystich Swietych. Do you know what is it?'

'No.'

'First of November. Day for Dead. Do you have this tradition in your country?'

'No.'

Stanislav walked to the window, leaned out, and pointed upward to the window from which the Nazis had flung an old Jewish woman in a wheelchair to the river below. Henry leaned out the window and looked at the spot where Stanislav said that her wheelchair had bounced into the river. Henry's eye began to twitch, and his stomach grumbled. Stanislav was humming a tune to himself. They went into the kitchen to have breakfast. Thank God, said Henry to himself, at last. The coffee was lukewarm and gritty and as thick as tar. The sausage was excellent. It reminded Henry of the German sausage you could buy in Magill's delicatessen on Clarendon Street. It reminded him of something else, but he didn't know what. Annemarie, perhaps.

The brothers went walking in the Market Square. Stanislav was concerned about his brother's leg. He suggested they could rest on a bench in the park but Henry insisted that they carry on. Henry was eager to get to the museum they had planned to visit. He could not understand why it had taken them so long to get there. Why should it take so long to buy tram tickets in a kiosk, to take a tram, to phone the airline in Warsaw? It simply did. This city seemed to dictate a pace that one could not exceed.

They stopped at the old city walls. In the same slow, grave tone that Jan had employed, Stanislav told Henry that Kraków was Poland's finest city. Henry felt mildly elated, despite a headache that was brewing in the back of his head and the near paralysis he felt from being so tired. He was, in those few minutes standing by the city's old walls, so enraptured by the peeling beauty of this small but monumental city, and so intrigued by his older, wiser brother that he felt an urge to fling his arms around him and bring him dancing through the noble little streets.

'Stanny—isn't life such a treasure?'

'I am sorry?'

'Let's go for a drink!'

'But the museum, it will be close—'

'First museum, then drink. OK?'

'Yes.'

Adjacent to a grey Baroque church was the Muzeum Czartoryskich. Attached to its doors, beneath a small plastic frame, was a warped image of Leonardo's 'Lady with the Ermine', the most honoured resident of the museum. The opening hours were pinned beneath her sleeve. It was two o'clock. The museum was not due to shut until three. Stanislav knocked loudly on the door. He burst a blister of brown paint. No answer came, so he knocked again. Still no answer came, so he knocked a third time. A man in a boiler suit and a bushy black beard answered the door. He looked at Stanislav and Henry, told them the museum was closed and shut the door. Henry protested: the museum was not supposed to close for another hour. Stanislav sighed, shrugged his shoulders, and said that there was nothing they could do. Henry could not believe his brother would tolerate this impudence. Did he not want to assert his right to entrance? Was it not his right to be in that museum, to saunter at his leisure about its rooms, to feast his eyes on the delectable Lady, the Lady of the Ear-mine as Stanislav had called her when they discussed her provenance over breakfast? Henry had been amazed that a Leonardo had found its way to Kraków. She was to be the quest of their first day together. How could Stanislav give up this easily? Listen Stan, he said, I'm going to make that bloody communist let us in. Henry pounded his fist against the blistered wooden door like a debt collector at the palace gates. Stanislav took a step back so that the guard would not see him. Does he not understand, thought Stanislav, that it is better and easier to be silent? Why draw attention to yourself like this? He hoped his brother was not mad. He hoped the door would not open, but it did. Henry bombarded the Lady's bodyguard, quite uselessly, in English.

How-dare-you-slam-the-door-in-our-faces-who-do-you-think-you-are-knocking-off-early-for-your-lunch-break-you-bloody-communist?!

The guard understood the last word. Zamkniete! he shouted thunderously through his beard, and slammed the door with all that he was worth. The building shuddered. Henry turned to Stanislav.

'I suppose that means closed?'

'Yes. Zamkniete means closed.'

Jesus, thought Henry, and I thought Ireland was bad.

In the square the pigeons warbled, pecked and fought. The flower vendors stood slouched behind their stalls, smoking into the customerless space. The brothers walked down Grodzka Street and turned onto Kanonicza Street by the Church of Saints Peter and Paul. There was not a soul on the cobbled Renaissance street. It was as warm as a fifteenth-century Italian afternoon.

'Henryk, we will go to Wawel Chapel, like the Lady with Ear-mine.'

'What did you say?'

'You see, that Lady with the Ear-mine was captivated, no, captured by the Nazis. General Frank took her there—you see—to Wawel Castle—there it was that the Nazi General stayed in the Occupation. And so he took with him our beautiful Italian lady.'

'Good Lord.'

'And then, later he took her to Bavaria to his home. But she was saved.'

'My goodness.'

'You had to see the giant swastikas on the Wawel Castle. I was child, as you know. It was not long after I left Lvov. The time you and Mama were in Lvov.'

Henry could not climb Wawel Hill with Stanislav. God only knows what he might uproot up there, Henry thought. He told Stanislav he would have to go back and rest.

'But there are many fine paintings in here, treasures of King Boleslaus, Saint Stanislav's sarcophagus—'

'I really don't feel that well. My leg, you know. It acts up.'

'Henryk, may I ask if it is a problem from the war?'

'What?'

'This leg. Is it from the war?'

'No. No, it is not from the war. May we go now?'

3

Why, thought Henry, do even the trees look unfamiliar? They looked emaciated, those trees. Post-communist trees. There was no breeze that evening. A red leaf fell down in front of Henry, floating east to west before he snatched it. There were black blotches on it. He put the leaf in his pocket, and walked on.

There's nothing familiar about this place, he thought, nothing at all. Red and black autumn leaves—what kind of an autumn is that? What kind of a place is this? A pint is what I need, a pint. Those bastards in Nesbitt's, they are my brothers. That is my home. He pictured himself slapping their backs in the bar. Home, he thought, I want to go home. My Ireland.

They were late for dinner, but Henry's flowers would charm the wife. Stanislav had forgotten that his brother's disabled leg would delay them. Besides, flowers had to be bought and churches, streets and monasteries had to be admired with a wave of the cane and lavish praise. How he talks, thought Stanislav, yet he says nothing. Nothing. He addresses my city, not me. He does not know what is important. Stanislav looked at his brother marching through the leaves with his silver-topped cane, like a pompous old general. He studied the limp. How did it happen? If it was not from the war, then what? An accident, a disease, a hostile Briton? He could not ask again. But when would he find out all that he had to know?

They reached block 6A of Prondnik Bialy. From a window on the fifth floor, Stanislav pointed to the horizon and said you could see the Tatra Mountains on a good day. It was not true, but it sounded good. Henry thought of the mountain folk that had taken them in on their flight from Lvov, and the pancakes that he smelt but never tasted in Zakopane. He asked Stanislav if the mountains were far away. One hundred kilometres, said Stanislav decisively, as if he had been expecting the question. We could go there, said Stanislav. I'd love to, said Henry. They climbed the stairs to Jan's apartment.

Jan ushered them into his apartment; his children peeped out through the kitchen door at the foreign man. Jan took Henry's jacket. Stanislav sat on a chair and unplucked the laces of his shoes. He slid them off and handed them to Jan, who took them to a concealed cloakroom and came back with two pairs of slippers dangling from his fingers. Poor man, thought Jan, with that artificial leg. He must have lost it in the war. He smiled, to show he understood. Henry smiled, and thought what a friendly, hospitable man Jan was. Stanislav said nothing to Jan. He had a new suspicion: that Henryk could understand Polish, that his forgotten Polish was a convenient guise for some devious strategy of espionage. How do I know he is my brother? Stanislav asked himself. I have not seen his documents. He knew he would have to find a way into Henry's pocket. Henry walked into the dining room with Jan, and handed the flowers to his wife. Stanislav lagged behind. He tiptoed back to the cloakroom where Jan had hung Henryk's jacket. He smothered the creak of the cloakroom door in a manufactured cough, reached in and found his brother's tweed coat. He dipped his hand into the inside pockets and took out a wallet, two pens and the passport. It was green with a hard back and had a golden harp embossed on the front with Ireland and Éire and Irlande printed below it. He remembered the stamps on his mother's letters. He opened the passport. There was a laminated photograph of Henryk on the second page. He was grinning like a clown. He turned the page. There was his mother's name. Elzbieta Malinska. So this was no impostor, after all.

Pani Pachocka darted in and out of the kitchen, carrying pots and pans and plates. She had spent a long afternoon preparing zurek soup, Russian dumplings, pork cutlets, coleslaw salad, beetroot salad and strawberry compote. She had laid the table with her prized linen tablecloth. The edges had been embroidered by her grandmother. She laid a bowl of zurek soup in front of the visitor, the visitor that was oblivious to the tablecloth, oblivious to the generations that had dined upon it, oblivious to Pani Pachocka as anything but a servant who bore food. Who does he think he is, trying to ingratiate himself with Stanislav Malinski? We are not fools. We can see he is no longer a Pole. When she took away his soup bowl there was still a little soup left at the bottom. He had not finished, but he smiled, and thanked her. She did not return his smile.

By the end of the first course Stanislav had not uttered a word in either Jan's or Henryk's direction. Jan could no longer bear to speak of furniture, buildings, weather and food. Henry was bored. How many times did he have to be told that Kraków was a city of superior culture and history? How much pity could he muster for the city that had suffered sixteen sieges and invasions, twenty-eight great fires, numerous catastrophic floods and even five earthquakes? A tirade against town planners seemed fitting, but it took an unexpected turn.

'... besides, what I'd like to say is that since you have been blessed with an elegant city like this ... I mean you should see Dublin, they have no pride in it, they've torn down Georgian buildings and replaced them with ugly offices, whole parts of our city are derelict, God knows Dublin looks like it was bombed in the war! They even built offices on medieval sites, would you believe. Whereas here, you have this beautiful city to feast your eyes upon every day, dare I say you should be grateful, despite the political turmoil of the past? What a glorious consolation this must have been, if, as you say, the rest of Poland's cities were bombed to dust in the war, and there are not two authentic bricks to rub together in the so-called old quarters of your other cities?'

Stanislav looked up. How did his brother dare refer to Poland's history like that? Was he proposing that a Gothic church or a Renaissance building could console a man as he waited in a queue for his measly monthly ration of butter? What the hell did Henryk know of communism? What did he know, on his safe, fat, green little island? I'll send you out to Nowa Huta, Stanislav thought, see what you think of it then.

'Henryk, you are not correct. The people of Kraków suffered as much as people of other cities in Poland. You do not understand. A building does not stop a man's hunger.'

Pani Pachocka put a pork cutlet in front of Henry. She hoped that this might stop him talking. She was sure she saw him wipe his finger on the tablecloth. Henry looked down at his cutlet and thanked her. He examined its coat of golden crumbs, feeling his brother's eyes on him all the time. Just like Mumsy, he thought, just like Mumsy. The guilt. He raised his eyes and met his brother's.

'I am aware, Stanislav, of that fact. I know that a building cannot prevent hunger. I only meant, the soul—'

'Soul? I do not understand this word.'

'You know, the thing which we all have but cannot see—'

'We have organisms inside us—stomach and heart and liver. I cannot see these.'

'But you know that they exist. They are material. But you do not know the soul exists, because it is not material.'

'So if it is not material then it is not my possession.'

'I only meant, I only wanted to say, that this is a beautiful city.'

'You have not seen all of Kraków.'

Henry leaned down to cut a square of cutlet. As he put it in his mouth, he thought of what Stanislav had said about the organs he had but could not see. He remembered a lesson in anatomy Doctor Hawkins had given him in the reading room of Holly Park. How Doctor Hawkins' cane had slid over the chart of glossy intestine, duodenum and pancreas, how like neatly stacked, undigested vegetables they looked. It seemed inconceivable that they lived inside a person. He remembered looking out onto the lawn at a decapitated Greek statue. A graceful hand held in it a bunch of grapes. Below, upon his femur, there was a hole. Through the hole a bluetit came and went: inside, it was hollow. We are hollow, Henry thought, and let his eyes glaze over for the rest of Doctor Hawkins' lesson. Back at the table, he took some beetroot salad. A drop of pink juice fell on the tablecloth, and the juice bled lilac into the linen. Pani Pachocka said something to Jan which Henry did not understand.

Stanislav knew, in the soul he denied he had, that it was his genteel, aching city that had given him the patience to endure Stalin, Gomulka, Gierek, all those fools. Once, in a thaw, he threw his arms around the corner of a building on Kanonicza Street in despair. They were allowed to keep their dignity, where men were not. They declared to the authorities their pride in embellishment: a flaking scroll, a drooping garland, a cluster of still, forgotten fruits on a Corinthian column. But Henryk did not have a right to know this. Henryk did not have a right to barge in and presume that all had been well, because it hadn't. There were things he would like to be told, before he disclosed any truths to his brother. The red toy train: did he get it in the end? Tell me that, before you tell me how I survived communism.

They drank coffee after their vodka. Pani Pachocka bustled them into the lounge area where there was a couch, identical to Stanislav's, and two chairs. She ripped the tablecloth from the table and soaked it in a bowl of bleach. She would always remember the foreigner for the beetroot stain. She would use the green cotton tablecloth the next time he came around.

'Henryk, please, some vodka.'

'Ah, yes. Good old Polish vodka. Haven't tasted it in fifty years!'

Stanislav pinned his eyes on him.

'You remember fifty years ago?'

'Oh yes! I was a veritable little vodka drinker. Don't you remember, Stanislav? Don't you remember lying around the orchards guzzling bottles of vodka on sunny days?'

Jan laughed, and slapped his palm down on the arm of his chair. Stanislav lit a cigarette.

'No, I don't remember.'

'It was a joke, Stanny, a joke. Good vodka, this.'

As the smoke curled out of his mouth, Henry saw that his brother's teeth were stained and old, that the third tooth from the front was missing. He had seen the early, milk-white teeth, but he had not seen these, stained by nicotine, age and coffee. He had not known this set of teeth.

'Henryk, may I ask, what is it you remember?'

Henry leaned his glass over the arm of the chair in the hope that Jan would see that it was empty. He noticed that everyone's glass was empty. He would answer, he could answer, when he had another swig. Oh come on Jan, don't be tight with the vodka!

He could feel what he had eaten thrusting its way through his intestines. He was not hollow, after all. The bluebells he had seen in the woods the day his mother died came back to him. Jan fumbled for the vodka.

'Mumsy. I remember Mumsy.'

'Who?'

'Mummy.'

'Mama. But of course you remember Mama. She died this year. Before, I am talking about before Irlandia. During the war. For example, a red toy train. You remember the red toy train?'

'The red train toy? I don't think so. Was it mine or yours?'

'Yours. Yours.'

'I'm afraid I don't remember it.'

Jan filled the glasses and they toasted to their health. There was a fog in Henry's head. He reached for a cigarette. He saw the word *papierosy* on the packet. Papierosy, he said to himself. Papierosy, paper-hoses, I am smoking paper-hoses, panty hoses, oh, la, what on earth am I doing here?

'It was the red train our grandfather gave you. You went with Mama to our home to get it back on the day the Germans came to Lvov. I did not go back with you. I stayed in the house of Jozef, our peasant friend. Because of this, because of this, we were separated. You don't remember?'

The words came through Henry's fog, like bees. He could not wave them away. They hovered over him and he knew they would sting.

'I am sorry, Stanislav, but I do not remember. I thought—our mother brought me back to the house with her to get her hats, I thought that was why, I always thought that was why.'

'Not so. It was the red toy train. Your red toy train.'

Jan filled up their empty glasses, and his own. He looked at Henry.

'We are Poles, you see,' Jan said to Henry, and he chuckled. 'That means we remember.'

4

Henry looked out the dining-room window as they were leaving the Pachockis. The leaves were baking quietly in the setting sun. The sky was a gritty, faded blue. The opposing house, in a skin of dust, seemed to gasp for a cloud of rain. He was drunk, and feeling generous. How could he repay the Pachockis for their hospitality? He would take them out to dinner. Pani Pachocka said she could not go. Did he not like the food? Did he think they could do better in the centre, in one of those sleazy restaurants that overcharged for everything? Jan said that they would be poisoned and besides, you had to wait hours for the food to arrive. Stanislav said nothing: his younger brother was showing off again. Jan then suggested that they spend an evening at the cabaret. He knew a good place on the market square. An image of Annemarie, at four, swinging her legs under a chair at the *Threepenny Opera* came to Henry's mind. He told his hosts he loved the theatre. He could thing of nothing better to do. But would they not like to eat out first? No, no, you will come back here to our home and you will eat with us. This is Poland, Pan Malinski, we always eat at home.

Stanislav had not seen Piotr Salicki since he left white chrysanthemums at Anna's funeral. He wished Anna was with him but Henry might have liked her a little too much. They had the theatre in common, after all.

In the morning, Henry's bag was delivered from Warsaw. Henry tipped the courier one hundred thousand zlotys. His Viyella shirt and his green cravat were back: he would wear them to the cabaret that evening. In his room, he put on his silk paisley dressing-gown and tied the cord around his waist. He was feeling better, with his clothes back. A man who leaves home naked does not travel well. But he still felt stiff and his head was clammy and his nose was blocked. He found, in the bottom of his valise, the perfume he had brought for Stanislav's wife, the boiled sweets and chocolate for his children.

He went to breakfast. There was Stanislav, suddenly so familiar, in the drudgery of his morning labours, clanking dishes in the sink. There, on the table, was the sausage and sheep's cheese and the bread with caraway seeds studded into its crust, just it had all been on the first day. This breakfast would be different. Henry's resurrected Red Toy Train would chug between them. Henry still could not remember the toy. Stanislav did not believe him. That was how it all started, with the red toy train. Nobody forgets a thing like that. Nobody forgets the day they last saw their brother, the day the Nazis came in tanks across the border. The kettle began to whistle. Stanislav ran to it, lifted it off the gas ring and poured the water over the coffee. He looked around, but Henry had gone. He set the coffee glasses down upon the table. Nobody could forget a thing like that. He peeped out at his jars of pickles, decided they still needed more time.

'Dzien dobry, Stanislav.'

'Dzien dobry, Henryk.'

'Look. Do you have any use for these?'

He handed him a withered Brown Thomas bag. Stanislav opened it and took out the bottle of Mystère de Rochas, the bags of sweets and the chocolate bars.

'For me?'

'If you like, Stanislav. I brought them for—your family—I mean, for children and your wife, if you, you know.'

'My wife is dead.'

'She's the dancer?'

'Yes. Anna. She was my wife.'

'No children.'

'No. She died too soon.'

Henry was afraid that his brother might weep.

'So let's have a bit of chocolate for breakfast then.'

'I'm sorry?'

'The chocolate. Let's eat it. We can drink the perfume later.'

'Yes, yes. Henryk, I must thank you very so much for your generosity. It is very kind. Dziekuje. Really, thank you.'

It was too late. Henry saw his brother's lower lip tremble, but he hid his tears this time. On their way to the kitchen, Henry saw him dab his eyes and blow his nose into his handkerchief.

Henry took a sip of coffee, trying not to scald his fingers on the thin glass. He should have waited for the grains to fall to the bottom of the glass, but that baked, comforting smell compelled him. The coffee had a chalky taste and the grains got stuck between his upper molars. It had been the same in the Pachocki house, and a *kawiarnia* they had visited the day before. Either they do not have filters, Henry speculated, or they do not like filtering. Stanislav saw his brother's fingers dance around his glass.

'It is too hot for you, Henryk?'

'Oh no, no, it's fine.'

He dislodged the coffee grains from his molars with his tongue.

'I can give you filizanka, you know, a little cup. Is it better?'

'Oh no, no it's fine.'

He swallowed the grains that had settled on his tongue.

'I am not such a hospital.'

'I beg your pardon?'

'I am not so—so—women are better for this job.'

'Nursing?'

'Yes, yes. For nursing. I am not so good.'

'So you chose architecture.'

'I am sorry?'

'You chose architecture, instead of nursing.'

'No, no. It is not job I mean. I'm not talking about this part of life. I mean now, here, with you. My hospital to you.'

'Hospitality, you mean.'

'Hospitality, I mean.'

'My God, Stanislav, that's not true at all. You've been very good to me. Very good to me indeed.'

'But I think, you know, women are better for this, to know which cup to use and so on, so on.'

'That's a bit old fashioned, isn't it, Stanislav?'

Henry pushed his glass of coffee aside, hoping the grains would make their way down through the thick, murky liquid.

'Henryk, do you mind I ask about your wife?'

He moved the plate of sausage across the table toward Henry. Henry plunged his molars into the soft meat, and swallowed.

'My wife—I—never had one.'

'Ah haah.'

It struck Henry then that in this other world he would have had to marry a Maureen Lindsay.

'However—I was once engaged.'

'With an Irish lady?'

'No, in fact not. She was German. Annemarie was her name. A beautiful German nymph.'

'German? Deutsche?'

'Yes, I had hoped that we would marry.'

'Ah, strange. I thought Irish woman—'

'Strange? To love and marry? What's strange?'

'Simply, Henryk, I did not expect this. It is a surprise.'

'You know something, Stanislav? You're very like our mother. Much more like her than I ever was.'

'How have you met this girl, in Germany?'

'No. Dublin.'

'She speaks English?'

'Yes.'

'You speak German?'

'Yes.'

Henry picked up his silver-topped cane and tapped it on the floor. He rubbed his thumb along the top of it and clenched his teeth. He reached for a slice of sausage and some cheese.

'What about this Anna, were you married for long?'

'Since after the war.'

'But you were very young just after the war.'

'Yes.'

'You married then?'

'No. I don't understand the question. That was when I met her on Vistula river. I met her on my twelfth birthday. But before, also, in school. I was still waiting for Mama and for you. Later I married Anna, when I knew Mama was not coming back.'

'But Stanislav, she asked you to come—to Ireland.'

'I asked her to come here. This is her country. Not Ireland.'

'Oh Lord. She waited. I think she waited all her life—'

'So I married Anna. We were in love, very happy. She was a dancer, such a fine dancer. She was at school in Warsaw. I saw her many times dance. She was a Sylph. Beautiful lady. Then she died, like the swans.'

Stanislav rose, and took the sausage away to the fridge. He poured his coffee down the sink and looked out the window at the swans. *I am betrayed. Everything I loved is gone, except this brother, this brother who grovelled for the enemy.* He ran water over the coffee grains, and watched them disappear down the sink. Back to the river.

'Do you like the theatre, Stanislav?'

'No. I do not like it. I never liked it.'

'So you like cabaret?'

'No. But you will like it. Good satiric.'

'Is it anything like Berlin cabaret?'

'No. Not like that. It is special Polish cabaret.'

5

In the garden of Wawel Castle, an old man was sweeping the leaves. He heard the tram ring past, and stopped. He looked at the pile of leaves in front of him and thought of winter. He glanced in at the Renaissance courtyard and saw a figure pass through an arcade. *The widow*, he thought to himself, *it's the widow again.* He lit a cigarette, spluttered out the smoke, and slung the brush over his shoulder. It was getting on. His wife didn't like him working these late hours. But he enjoyed working those last, fading hours of the day. As he walked past the golden cupola of Sigismund's Chapel, he slipped his cap off. He had no hair, and his ears stuck out. The golden scallops of the dome, asleep under the grey night, were like the scales of Krak's old dragon. The old man chuckled to himself, remembering the tar he once poured over it weeks before the Nazis came, how he and his father and his cousins had saved the gold. The tram rang out again. He put his cap back on and strolled home.

Henry, Stanislav and Jan got out of the tram where Grodzka Street intersects with All Saints'. On the Market Square they passed a restaurant with outdoor seating. A warm blast of air brought the smell of grilled meat with it. Henry sniffed, and thought how nice it would have been to eat under a canopy, with the balmy evening all around them, and a trio of Romanian musicians scuttling from table to table. As they rushed past Mariacki Cathedral, Henry saw a flock of stern-faced nuns turn the corner. They walked on past the closed, shuttered shops and the receding archways. Henry heard a snatch of jazz through the archway, and he wondered were the nuns off on the tear.

Henry's cold was worse. He had cold sweats and a stiff, dry cough. His head was blocked. People's faces looked strange to him: noses protruded and extended, eyes bulged, skin seemed to him like ugly, puckered pig meat. He felt dizzy in the ticket queue, and he had to steady himself on the banister. In the window of the ticket office, he raised a hand with three fingers to a lady with a bag of fruit on her head. Her upper lip curled as she shoved the tickets under the window. There was no change. Henry managed a hoarse *dziekuje* and staggered away, with his arm shaking on his cane and his wooden leg creaking like an old ship.

Henry's good leg shook as he descended the cold, stone spiral stairs. *Thank God for my little cane, thank God.* The three men entered Jama Michailika, the Cave of Michael, for an evening of cabaret. Its ceiling was low and bent, the light was muted by thick smoke. There was a low murmur coming from them. Henry found himself in a room of busy ghosts in the heart of an old, dry, shipwreck at the bottom of the sea. That *creaking*. He belched. He forgot his manners in the underworld. Outside, the sky rumbled, and threatened, but no storm came.

The walls of Jama had antlers, bearskins, gilt braided military tunics, spiked helmets, Russian maces, medals, daggers, bisque-headed dolls with empty sockets, velvet doublets, embroidered waistcoats, a ballerina's tutu (with an overlay of silver lace), portraits, caricatures, photographs and posters for the cabaret's more notable post-Stalin performances. It was like one of those hidden storerooms in a museum that no one ever sees. Henry saw the clutter of centuries pinned upon the walls, a sea of precious junk that gave the blasted little cave no sense of time at all. It could have been an alchemist's den, a de-sanctified crypt, a medieval banquet, a Turkish bazaar, the lumber-room of a dead aristocrat, an opium-den, the treasure hoard of a miserly privateer. Pale and weak, he stared at its walls and swayed, still seasick. There, between a mannequin's leg and a shield embossed with a dragon's head, was a dagger lying across two nails. It had plated mounts and an orange grip with the Third Reich eagle at its base. He jumped away from it, and then looked up. He saw a ballerina suspended by white rope with her arms spread out, swimming through the air. *A heavy white fish*, thought Henry, *but I like the eyebrows, they're well plucked*. She disappeared again among the tunics and the helmets, the cracked cymbals and the outgrown clocks.

Stanislav looked around for a free table. He saw the backs of men hunched over their drink, griping about politics, and wives, and money. He saw them as a pack, a drove, a herd that, collectively, had prowled around his Anna, looked up her skirt, and by it tugged her away from him forever. Their leader was the tall, gaunt idol in the corner table below the stage, sitting under Anna's tutu. Piotr Salicki had already seen him. He found a table at the back of the club, and sat facing his brother, with his back to the Master of Ceremonies. He tapped his fingers on the table and waited to be served. Stanislav hoped that his brother had not come for the women. It was a literary cabaret, not a Berlin orgy.

Jan nodded his way through the crowd, looking for pretty faces. He could not help himself, when it came to women. He loved to raise their light hands to his mouth, to skid his lips over the backs of them, looking down their cleavage and into their eyes. He was a perfect gentleman. He felt his wife pulling at the flaps of his jacket; he would wake up beside her with a pounding headache. As he was squeezing between the backs of two chairs on his way to the toilet, he saw the woman he had met in the train station a few days before. *The one with the eyelashes and three bags.* Her eyes had turned to stone and her smile had frozen. Why was she back from Prague so soon? Was that her husband she was with? He dashed past and in the toilet, under the glaring light and in the stinging smell of piss, he resolved, as he relieved himself, to catch her eye as he went past her table. There could be no harm in that, surely?

Through all that mucus, Henry could smell mould. *Why? Why is it so damp among the revellers and the ghouls?* He swayed in his ship. He sneezed, and wished he could go back to land. *I am not a fish, not a fish.* He glanced over at the next table where a woman with a snout sat drinking from a goldfish bowl. *There is a smell of fish.* Henry remembered the story of the woman on Moore Street who shouted 'FRESH FISH!', and under her breath, said 'God forgive me.' *Fresh fish, fresh fish, God Jesus Christ Almighty is that Maureen Lindsay in the corner, no, no, it's a fish, another mouldy,*

scaly fish. I know where I am, I know where I am, I'm at the cabaret,
down a few flights of stairs that I'll never get up again, they'll have to
carry me out on a stretcher, I'm suffocating in the smell of fish. Christ,
the dagger's glinting at me, who owned it? Who gutted fish with it?
Jesus, what if the Teutonic Knights are here, what if they've found
their way to the underworld?

Anna's tutu, the one she wore for *La Sylphide*, hung, like a giant shell in a Museum of Natural History, over Piotr Salicki's head. That costume had encased her body, and she had donated it, like a lung or a liver, for the progress of (Stanislav deemed it) debauchery and cheap thrill. *All your booty hanging on the walls! All the slaves you exploited and expelled!* He saw Anna's shape in the moth-eaten costume, and remembered her white legs in arabesque, in jetté, plié and pirouette. He remembered the frozen little girl on the frozen Vistula in a blue scarf, inviting him for sausage. The muff, the fall, the little girl. He took a mouthful of vodka and remembered his mother, the first woman he had ever lost. He looked at Henry: she had been *his* mother too. She had nurtured them both, and brought them, one after the other, into this world. But what did they have in common, apart from that? Where could they find their sunburnt children's souls again? War had stunned those out of them. Stanislav looked at his brother. He took another mouthful of vodka. He thought of his mother again. His mother and his brother. The last time they had been together was in Lvov, a place to which he had never returned. They would have to go back, together, he and Stanislav. That was the only way. That was the only way for them to be brothers again. He took another mouthful of vodka, lit a cigarette, and tapped his brother on the shoulder.

'Henryk, I have thought. It is time to go to Lvov.'

'Stan-is-lav. I'm not well. There's an awful smell of fish in here. Can you hear me?'

'You want to go?'

'Oh no, no, no. Loving it here. When's the show?'

'It is late. Henryk, you do not understand. I ask if you want to go to Lvov, with me.'

'Where?'

'Lvov. Where we were born.'

'Oh no we can't do that we might bump into a Teutonic Knight, oh no there'd be ghosts out there, Stanny, I'm not well and there's this awful smell of fish …'

'You want to go?'

'Oh no, I'm loving it, really.'

'Look, Henryk—it is beginning.'

When Henry turned to face the stage, he felt blood rush to his head and he heard it gurgle, as if he had been submerged into a pot of boiling water. He was aware of drums and a red glow somewhere. His vision came back, blurred. When the audience clapped he thought the storm had broken and it had rained in the old ship. At last, he thought, I am gasping for a drop of water. He took the glass of clear liquid in front of him and threw its contents down his throat. The vodka scalded him. All he wanted was water. A simple, clear glass of water. But the show went on. Rows of candelabra lit the stage. Red cloth was draped over the floor. A suit of armour hung beside a mannequin in a Hussar Captain's blue and gold tunic. Henry saw them hang like dead men from the rafters. A little bell rang out at the end of man's long arm. He was tall, sinuous and black against the red. His clerical bell seemed demonic. Singing. Women in long white robes with Renaissance faces rising to crescendo, crashing down, *piano,*

piano, whispers, gone again into the dizziness. A huge thin man came out of the dark. He had big, sad black eyes that looked hungrily at Henry. He was in rags. He moved along the stage with a staff taller than himself. He was an old Jew, Henry saw, with the face of old Mr Schveetheart Tailor moving in the wind. He had no right to shut his eyes, but he did. His old boat creaked again. Stanislav whispered something to him about a green balloon and the Berlin Wall, but he could not understand. The music bellowed out, just drums. The air softened, with harps, was it a harp? Or a lute or a lyre? An angel came, moved across the stage with a long red candle like St Cecilia, singing like a flute, but went so fast away from him, she was the only thing that soothed, and out came those menacing bastards in their Nazi uniforms, there, there on the stage, was the dwarf and the clown of his dream, with the Red Toy Train running between them like a messenger, and there hanging from the rafters was his mother and his father, there, beside him was Stanislav, his brother. He tried to put his head under the tablecloth, but it was too late. The cabaret was over.

6

Stanislav let his brother sleep. He looked out the kitchen window at the river: the sun gleamed over a patch of oil. The only swan he could see had its head sunk in the water. He turned his back to the window, and began to make his brother's breakfast. He laid the sausage, sheep's cheese and bread on a tray. He made tea instead of coffee. He peered in at the trapped, immobile vegetables in the sitting room to see how they were faring: just the same, just the same as the first time he had seen them in the cellar, during the war.

'Dzien dobry, Henryk.'

There came no answer from the bed. Henry opened an eye, and tried to say something to the voice that spoke, that had spoken like a giant bear. He had a whole, coherent sentence formed in his head (*Good morning, Bear, I'm not so well today but I'm hungry, I'm hungry, could you fetch me a sandwich or a bowl of soup?*), but all that came out was a short, mid-pitched whistle, followed by a groan.

'Sniadanie, Henryk. Break-fast. After, medicine. Is it OK?'

He set the tray down on his brother's belly. Out of the corner of his eye, Henry saw a bird fly past the widow. Little bird, said Henry to the bird, if you're flying west, send them my best, tell them I died with a plate of sausage on my belly, tell them I came home at last, tell them—

'Henryk, can you sit, please?'

He was a large boulder. *It would take ten men to move me, you old bear.* He opened his eyes a fraction wider to see what had been brought for him to eat. Stanislav leaned down, lodged his hands under his brother's armpits and propped him up against the pillows.

Stanislav fed his brother the sausage slices and the sheep's cheese. He dabbed the corners of his brother's mouth with a napkin. Henry's wooden leg was propped up against the bedside table, like part of a broken puppet. He wanted to speak to Stanislav. *I am rotting in this stinking weed of sea, in rancid fish, it is a bad case of calenture, Dr Hawkins, a bad case of calenture, you must bring me back to shore, I cannot bear it any longer, besides I must talk and he's not here for long you know, look look I saw the cat leap down the headless statue, he's eating all the birds, he's eating all the birds, they're trapped little birds in a hollow place, so much bloody mud, Doctor will you take me out of here, it's so dark and there's an awful smell of fish …*

Stanislav saw his brother's lips move over silent words. He felt his forehead. It was burning. He left the building and took a tram to the central post office, and from there he called a private doctor. He waited three and a half hours for a doctor who said he would be there in ten minutes. He sat by his brother's bed, trying to trace his brother's words through the slur. The doctor came and prescribed a course of antibiotics. The Kraków air had done it. He handed Stanislav the bill with the prescription and left.

Stanislav let his brother sleep, but he was afraid that he would never wake. He suspected that this fever was his brother's due. It was part of Henryk's redemption. *Not that I am religious, no, not at all, but we do all have to do our penance, and that includes myself. Look at him there, as limp and helpless as a child. There is my younger brother Henryk, the one who used to leap about the schoolroom after butterflies. I hope he has not come back here to die.*

Henry did not open his eyes for three days. Stanislav paced the rooms smoking cigarette after cigarette, enmeshed in smoke that made his throat swell and his bottom lip sting. There would be no time left, if Henryk did not recover. He would not be able to ask his questions. He did not leave the apartment. It was to Pani Mizera, the neighbour, that he turned, though he had vowed to avoid her while Henry was in the house. She made the boys dinner in her fetid kitchen. She boiled meat and cabbage and hammered potatoes to dry pulp with her wooden mallet. Stanislav brought trays of steaming, beaten food to his brother's bedside and fed him with a spoon. There is your retribution.

There, but it is not all your fault. My city has poisoned you with its dirty fog.

Henry, in the meantime, had left his boat and come to shore. He lay on the beach like an exhausted Gulliver. When he was hungry he was fed with a light aluminium spoon. Fennel, red cabbage, greasy mashed potato, horseradish sauce, threads of dry meat, syrupy fruit juices were spooned into his mouth by some devoted hand. Soft, puréed food that he did not have to chew, that slithered down his throat.

Henry's delirium had brought him to Lvov. He met warped images of the days that he had fled. They performed and re-performed their grotesque repertoire, and he could not rest. In his sleep he was fed vodka by the hand of Hilbig and Hilbig breathed in his ear like a bellows full of rotten, glaucous phlegm. He licked vodka from a spoon. His teeth were brown and yellow and his tongue was green. Henry saw the clown and the dwarf at the end of his bed, filing their nails, stroking and fawning and drooling over their Masssster. Henry said: I am afraid. But nobody heard, because his lips never moved, and the spoon came back, shovelling his mother's food down, back down into the dark. He saw his father at his desk, mixing ink in his samovar, smoking long, hollow pens and smiling benevolently through a window he could not see, but that he knew was there. He waved to them and heard music—was it Liszt, that beautiful piano?—and Mr Schveetheart Tailor held up a tailcoat made of blue and white stripes and he smiled, and behind him, out of the cupboards behind him, came the Jewish people who had lived around him in Lvov, young children and old men, all came to see Henry in his bed, crowding the room so that he thought the house would cave in, because he knew that they were heavy, he knew what they had lost, he knew what they were looking for, and then he saw his mother peering through the window at him but she refused to come in. In the far, far distance, beyond the field of blazing sunflowers, he saw a little red train chugging toward the horizon and above, the stork.

On the fourth day, Henry ate with a knife and a fork. Pani Mizera came to see him, and nattered by his bedside about her husband's consumption, her rheumatism, his collapsed lung, her skin disorder, all the quirks of her daily sufferings, all the perils of old age. Henry nodded and smiled. He found her attentive banter a comfort. He saw before him a simple old woman. Not a ghoul or a fish, but a simple old woman. The delirium had passed. He could not understand a word she said. He listened to her, as a child that has not yet learned to speak might listen. The intonation was gentle, the racing consonants a puzzle. Her monologue was a soothing whisper, interrupted only by sporadic hisses of laughter which would crease her face entirely. He had been grateful for her cooking, and, as she left, he smiled feebly and said *dziekuje*, which made the old lady erupt in laughter once again.

Henry saw the tree-top outside the window and saw that the rich colours had faded, in his absence, to a uniform rusty-brown. He wanted to reach out of the open window and nab one of the leaves, as dry as paper, to crunch it in his fist. But he was still too weak.

He was aware of his brother pottering about in the next room. That thin, drawn silver-haired man was his brother. He had ministered to his every need in the last three days. His brother was silent, then, but for the sound—it was very faint, but he was sure he could hear it—of a pen scratching across a page. The red toy train: what nonsense is he on about? Can we not embrace, and make our meeting festive, like other reunited brothers? He could not picture the red toy train. He saw Stanislav in his grey shorts standing on a pile of rubble: the King of Memory. Somewhere under the rubble was the red toy train. Battered but there. Maybe.

Did Stanislav know? Did Stanislav know what he had seen in the room in the last three days? Had he heard him scream when the Jews came out of the cupboards toward him, in the bed? Had he yelled out Hilbig's name? Anything could have spilled out. All his well kept secrets. Henry shivered, and sneezed. He turned on his side and fell asleep for an hour.

Stanislav came in at three o'clock with a chicken cutlet and some cherry compote that Pani Mizera had concocted below. He nudged his brother.

'Henryk, it is lunch. How do you feel?'

'Mmm. Breadcrumbs. Starving. Absolutely starving. Thank you.'

'You are better now, I think.'

'Yes. I am. Much better. No more delirium.'

'I'm sorry?'

'Ravings. Visions. Illusions of the eye.'

'Ah. Majaczenie.'

'My-achennay.'

'Yes. You were a little mad. I was sorry for you, Henryk.'

Stanislav left the room and Henry ate alone. He stared at his chicken cutlet. Which word, from the thousands of words there were, was he to choose? He chewed his cutlet. Good chicken, it was good chicken. He could have eaten the same again.

Stanislav was sitting at the bureau, writing. It was outrageous, he had decided, that he should have to suffer this dereliction. Did

the authorities have no consideration for its citizens? He took his
pen up again, and began to write.

Dear Sirs,
  *I am writing with the intention of filing a complaint, regarding
the condition of No. 3A, St Bronislav's Street …*

He paused again. It was appalling that he had to live at the
top of a flight of tatty stairs. God knows, his brother could have
fallen down and killed himself. It was high time something was
done about those stairs. For heaven's sake, where was the freedom
they had been promised, what sort of democracy was this? Life
had not improved at all. It was even worse. God knows, he was
still waiting for the telephone he had ordered just after he had
married Anna. Administration could not get away with letting
people live in slums! He would have picked up the telephone and
given them what they deserved. But he had no telephone. He
lifted up his pen to write again and before he reached the page he
stopped. He heard his brother calling him. He went into the
room.

7

The white nylon curtains blew in the wind. The central heaters
gurgled. Henry's tongue felt dry. Under the bedclothes, his hands
were clasped together, as if in prayer. A twitch began to beat
under his left eye, like a finger tapping. He licked beads of sweat
from above his upper lip. The taste of salt. He wished he had not
done it. He wished he had not called his brother to the room. He

closed his eyes and tried to picture a street in Dublin: Dame Street. Broad, grand Dame Street, with Trinity College at its crown. But it would not come to him. He summoned it again: a creased, jaded postcard arrived. Why, he thought, does my Alma Mater fail me now?

Stanislav came into the room. He saw his brother in the bed. His brother. His bed. He saw the wooden leg propped against a chair with a pile of clothes thrown over the back of it. He saw his brother's shoes at the end of the bed. Touching at the heels, they made a 'V' shape as a clown might stand. He looked at the curtain blowing in and noticed his brother's ties and cravats hanging from the curtain rail. Pieces of him were everywhere. He seemed so much nicer like this: dismantled. Was he hungry? Did he have a headache? Was his temperature rising? Did he need the basin? Damn administration, he said to himself, my brother will never get down those stairs.

'Stanislav. Do you remember the day I left with our mother?'

Stanislav folded his arms, and perched himself at the end of the bed. The edges of his mouth turned down, and he kept his eyes to the floor. He tightened his arms around his chest.

'Stanislav?'

He breathed through his nostrils. A faint whistling sound came through it. Like Aunt Magdalena, like Aunt Magdalena. He could not move his mouth. He found himself at the door of an empty church, with a Baroque altar behind him. A sweet, sticky smell loitered in the aisles. Could it have been his communion? No matter. Would he let Henryk in? Would he let him atone? And Mama, did she leave without atonement? I am not religious, of course, he said to himself, but we must all do our penance, and that includes myself.

'Stanislav. Please, answer me.'

'I cannot.'

'All right, all right, I'll stop.'

The scraping of the metal curtain rings on the rail, after a breeze. A skip being lowered into a concrete yard across the river. The distant hum of cars, and a brief ring of a tram on the bridge. The low sun, hanging behind a net of filthy cloud. A single swan gliding down the river with a yellow stain on its wing. In the room, nothing moved and there was no sound. Each brother waited for the other to speak. Quiet in the room, but the heaters gurlged.

'We will go to Lvov, Henryk. Then can we talk.'

'No. I'm not going there.'

'It is our home.'

'I came here to see you, not some derelict old house.'

'You are afraid?'

'No. It's a waste of time. That's all. We can talk here, we're talking here, aren't we, for God's sake?'

'Henryk. Seven days and we say nothing. Nothing. You are a wall.'

In the garden of Wawel Castle, an old man was sweeping the leaves. He leaned down, picked up an armload of dry leaves from the pile he had swept, and dropped them into a plastic container. Out of the corner of his eye, under a laurel bush, he saw a half-drunk bottle of vodka lying on its side. He picked it up and twisted the cap open. Vodka. But God knows some devil could have put it there as poison for the tempted. He screwed the cap back on and tossed the bottle into the container with the leaves. He remembered the night he spied on a drunken German soldier there, in Wawel gardens, during the war, from a tree by the river bank. He had been painting, that was it. Some little squirt was nosing about under the tree and he climbed up beside him. He chuckled. He would tell his wife the story when he got home. He swept the rest of the leaves up the path, and took the tram home.

'Do you know what is important, Henryk? All the time you laugh and joke and everything for you is so funny—'

'I'm not joking now, am I? I'm sick.'

'Please—I am not being rude. I only think, to go to Lvov could—I mean, it is our cemetery.'

'I will never go there.'

'You are afraid. I see you are afraid. The past, I know the past. It is like sleeping monster. Like the dragon under Wawel. You know this dragon?'

'You told me about him the other day.'

'Yes—the past is like this sleeping dragon.'

'Not sleeping. Dead.'

'For me it sleeps and I see it is for you—not dead. Not yet. You are afraid.'

'How the hell can you see? You don't know me.'

'I am your brother-'

'Fifty years, Stanislav, Fifty years.'

'Forty-nine.'

'Whatever. A hell of a long time.'

'I am sorry, Henryk. You are not well. You need something, maybe?'

'I don't need anything.'

Stanislav was still perched at the edge of the bed. All his weight was on his legs. It grew dark outside. They heard a tram ringing over the far bridge. The park keeper was in that tram, going home to his wife, preparing the story for her. Herr Feldwebel had smashed the bottle of vodka over the soldier's head, and he had seen the two boys perched in the tree, and ran at them waving his baton over his head, and his jowls were wobbling, and the swastika flag snapped in the wind, and the boys fled home with Heinkels droning over their heads ...

'You know, don't you, what happened in Lvov?'

'No. I know nothing.'

'Nothing. Are you sure? '

'It was a prison for you and Mama. Was some Nazi sergeant there?'

'What else do you know about the Nazi?'

'Nothing.'

'How do you know?'

'We had guessed it. Jozef said the Nazis were there already when you and Mama reached the house. He said the devils were already there, but Mama, she went in. And you. You also went in.'

'How did he know?'

'He was there. Then he came back and he told me. He did not go in, you see. He was not so stupid.'

'Stanislav. Do not ask me to go back. It makes me ill, the thought of it.'

'Why?'

'Why? Because it just does, that's why.'

'I had impression it was not so bad. You were at home, in our family home. I was sent to Kraków, to this place, with Aunt Magdalena. She was witch, you know. Czarnowieka. She was crazy, completely mad woman, Catholic woman ... for last years she couldn't even speak she was so crazy. Eyes like—'

'I'd have preferred to be in Kraków.'

'Here? In Kraków? Why? No food.'

'You think I feasted in Lvov? I dug potatoes from the earth with my raw hands in the bitch cold … there was nothing to eat … it was a barren desert. Not a home anymore, but the pulp of a home, the battered, empty, beaten pulp. Not a home, Stanislav. An occupied zone. The eagles' nest. They burned those landscapes—do you remember the funny naïve ones we had?'

'Yes, there was one with a falling house—I remember it. Grandmother hated it.'

'They burned them because they were painted by a biologically inferior hand … I saw them burn in a fire out the back of the house. I saw the paint drip off the canvas, I remember my cheeks burning. Then they put the Führer's picture in the empty space …'

'You remember so much, Henryk, I did not know you remembered so much.'

The sweet, sticky odour in the church came back to Stanislav. From the altar, a waft of candle smoke descended, and mingled with the sweeter odour. He moved down the cold flagstones of the nave. His footsteps sounded like drops of water plopping into a deep well. He came to the door, and looked back at the Blessed Mother doting on her Son, with the folds of her blue veil loosely cloaking Him, and he opened the door. A shaft of light wedged in the door, brightening a slice of the church. Stanislav glowered at the sun and held out his hand to his younger brother whom he could not see but he knew was there.

'Do you know what he did to us, Stanislav?'

'Who?'

'Hilbig. Hilbig. Hilbig, the bastard Hilbig.'

He nibbled the underside of his finger. He would have to do

it. He took his brother's hand and told him what he had never told another man. He told him everything there was to tell. Stanislav turned to see the swans outside, but they were not there. Henry told him, he told him everything.

He spoke of Hilbig and as he did he remembered the eggy smell of him, he felt it sailing up his nostrils and out his ears. To speak of that man. To speak of Hilbig who had sent the Jewess to her death in the orchard and sent a man to Belzec with a blue star for stealing meat. Never mind, never mind that Hilbig ate the horses from the stables in that bitch of a winter in '43. A thousand blue stars for you, a thousand blue stars for eating all the horses from the stables. To bring that man into the room, with his brother there. There he was, breathing between them. Egg breath and the leather hands and the clean white fingernails. A man who said his prayers every day, a man who said his prayers and sang *Stille Nacht* at Christmas. The heel of his boot in Mama's chest. Elizabet, my little treasure, my little cat. His eagle knife that chopped the toe, red in the snow. Pani Mizera in the kitchen, banging pots, below. Hilbig. The pots. Mama. Pani Mizera flinging the cutlery in the drawer. The trambell ringing outside. A bird singing. Was it a lark? Was that a lark in the birch tree? Henry told his brother everything. And Stanislav moved to the window, laid his elbows on the sill, quietly. Not a sound out of him, not a sound. Then he turned to Henry and he said: 'You and Mama left me.'

'There was no time.'

Stanislav made a fist in his palm and shut his eyes and out of the scrunched lids of them came tears. But you could not hear him cry. The bird sang in the birch and downstairs Pani Mizera piled up her crockery in the cupboard.

'And the red toy train?'

'Hats, Stanislav, hats and silver.'

Stanislav came up to his brother and leaned over the bed. His eyes were wide and his eyebrows were raised up on his forehead, like seagulls flying over the sea in Galway, Henry thought, where I held my *schatz* Annemarie in the wind. Stanislav leaned down and said 'We must go back to Lvov', with his fists all bony at his sides, in a sort of whisper. Henry closed his eyes but he could hear the breath singing through his brother's nose, and smelled the odour of his sweat drying in his gabardine jacket. He closed his mouth and swallowed. He would not go back. He wanted soup. Would Pani Mizera bring him soup?

8

They walked by the Vistula. It was a cloudless day, and the river was still. Stanislav looked at the swans, and asked his brother if they had swans where he came from and he told them they did, and that they were much the same there. They strolled on and passed the new supermarket by the bridge and continued along the river. Stanislav stopped and stared back at the swans. You know, he said, all that time they knew nothing, the swans knew nothing about the war or Stalin or that I looked at them every day from my window.

They took the number six tram to the Central Station. The 15.20 train to Lublin would leave from platform three. They already had their tickets. A bus would take them from Lublin to Lvov. Because there was no time for visas, Jan had made a phone call to a friend who worked at the Polish border post, who knew someone on the Soviet side. The trambell rang out as they passed Wawel Castle and Stanislav noted the rock on the riverside where Anna had first skated over to him. On his twelfth birthday, in 1946. Henry looked at his watch. Five past three, five past three.

They took window seats in the train compartment. There were no sunflowers in the fields and Henry saw no storks. He watched the flat fields race past the window like flying carpets. He saw the silver birches and heard his mother whisper *brzoza* into his ear. Stanislav brought tea and tripe soup from the restaurant car when they were an hour from Lublin. The bald man by the door seat had begun to snore. Stanislav heard his father's clock tick in his mind. There is no time left. He saw himself plucking a red apple in the orchard, warm from the autumn sun. That was what he wanted, just a simple apple from the orchard. To begin again, to begin again.

But there were no apples. The orchards of the manor had been hacked to stubs. Kolkzoz no. 187 had been an orphanage for twenty years. Henry and Stanislav were greeted by children at the door of their old home and the matron brought them into the rooms of the old house which were stacked, white wall to white wall, with bunk-beds. The floors were covered in blue linoleum, the ceilings had fluorescent lights hanging from rusty chains.

In the office, the matron showed them the only piece of original furniture that remained. It was Hilbig's black leather armchair. She sat down in it and offered Henry and Stanislav two chairs on the other side of the desk. She clasped her hands together and outlined to them the bureaucratic complexities of reclaiming lost private property. She was very polite, and an assistant brought them tea. They thanked the matron and told her the purpose of their visit was not to claim the house. They went outside and stood on the veranda, looking out at the tower blocks by the old paddocks. As they were leaving, the children came out to the front door and waved to them. The brothers waved back once. Henry limped ahead of his brother, and Stanislav kept looking back. He saw a stork fly over the old house. He called Henry, but his brother didn't hear. He was at a kiosk by the tower blocks, buying cigarettes.